The
Island of Faith

MARGARET E. SANGSTER

1ˢᵗ WORLD
LIBRARY
Literary Society

The Island of Faith

Margaret E. Sangster

© 1st World Library – Literary Society, 2005
PO Box 2211
Fairfield, IA 52556
www.1stworldlibrary.org
First Edition

LCCN: 2004195648

Softcover ISBN: 1-4218-0470-0
Hardcover ISBN: 1-4218-0370-4
eBook ISBN: 1-4218-0570-7

Purchase *"The Island of Faith"*
as a traditional bound book at:
www.1stWorldLibrary.org/purchase.asp?ISBN=1-4218-0470-0

The Island of Faith
contributed by Tim, Ed & Rodney
in support of
1st World Library Literary Society

To M's M and Chance

CONTENTS

I

INTRODUCING - THE SETTLEMENT HOUSE

There is a certain section of New York that is bounded upon the north by Fourteenth Street, upon the south by Delancy. Folk who dwell in it seldom stray farther west than the Bowery, rarely cross the river that flows sluggishly on its eastern border. They live their lives out, with something that might be termed a feverish stolidity, in the dim crowded flats, and upon the thronged streets.

To the people who have homes on Central Park West, to the frail winged moths who flutter up and down Broadway, this section does not exist. Its poor are not the picturesque poor of the city's Latin quarter, its criminals seldom win to the notoriety of a front page and inch-high headlines; it almost never produces a genius for the world to smile upon - its talent does not often break away from the undefined, but none the less certain, limits of the district.

It is curious that this part of town is seldom featured in song or story, for it is certainly neither dull nor unproductive of plot. The tenements that loom, canyon-like, upon every side are filled to overflowing with human drama; and the stilted little parks are so teeming with romances, of a summer night, that only the book of the ages would be big enough to hold them - were they written out! Life beats, like some great wave, up the dim alleyways - it breaks, in a shattered tide, against rock-like doorways. The music of a street band, strangely sweet despite its shrillness, rises triumphantly above the tumult of pavement vendors, the crying of babies, the shouting of small boys, and the monotonous voices of the womenfolk.

In almost the exact center of this district is the Settlement House - a brown building that is tall and curiously friendly. Between a great hive-like dwelling place and a noisy dance-hall it stands valiantly, like the soldier of God that it is! And through its wide-open doorway come and go the girls who will gladly squander a week's wage for a bit of satin or a velvet hat; the shabby, dull-eyed women who, two years before, were care-free girls themselves; the dreamers - and the ones who have never learned to dream. For there is something about the Settlement House - and about the tiny group of earnest people who are the heart of the Settlement House - that is like a warm hand, stretched out in welcome to the poor and the needy, to the halt in body and the maimed in soul, and to the casual passer-by.

II

THE QUARREL

"They're like animals," said the Young Doctor in the tone of one who states an indisputable fact. "Only worse!" he added.

Rose-Marie laid down the bit of roll that she had been buttering and turned reproachful eyes upon the Young Doctor.

"Oh, but they're not," she cried; "you don't understand, or you wouldn't talk that way. You don't understand!"

Quite after the maddening fashion of men the doctor did not answer until he had consumed, and appreciatively, the last of the roll he was eating. And then -

"I've been here quite as long as you have, Miss Thompson," he remarked, a shade too gently.

The Superintendent raised tired eyes from her plate. She was little and slim and gray, this Superintendent; it seemed almost as though the slums had drained from her the life and colour.

"When you've been working in this section for twenty years," she said slowly, "you'll realize that nobody can ever understand. You'll realize that we all have animal traits - to a certain extent. And you'll realize that quarrelling isn't ever worth while."

"But" - Rose-Marie was inclined to argue the point - "but Dr. Blanchard talks as if the people down here are scarcely human! And it's not right to feel so about one's fellow-men. Dr. Blanchard acts as if the people down here haven't *souls*!"

The Young Doctor helped himself nonchalantly to a second roll.

"There's a certain sort of a little bug that lives in the water," he said, "and it drifts around aimlessly until it finds another little bug that it holds on to. And then another little bug takes hold, and another, and another. And pretty soon there are hundreds of little bugs, and then there are thousands, and then there are millions, and then billions, and then -"

The Superintendent interrupted wearily.

"I'd stop at the billions, if I were you," she said, "particularly as they haven't any special bearing on the subject."

"Oh, but they *have*" said the doctor, "for, after a while, the billions and *trillions* of little bugs, clinging together, make an island. They haven't souls, perhaps," he darted a triumphant glance at Rose-Marie, "but they make an island just the same!"

He paused for a moment, as if waiting for some sort of comment. When it did not come, he spoke again.

"The people of the slums," he said, "the people who drift into, and out of, and around this Settlement House, are not very unlike the little bugs. And, after all, *they do help to make the city*!"

There was a quaver in Rose-Marie's voice, and a hurt look in her eyes, as she answered.

"Yes, they are like the little bugs," she said, "in the blind way that they hold together! But please, Dr. Blanchard, don't say they are soulless. Don't -"

All at once the Young Doctor's hand was banging upon the table. All at once his voice was vehemently raised.

"It's the difference in our point of view, Miss Thompson," he told Rose-Marie, "and I'm afraid that I'm right and that you're - not right. You've come from a pretty little country town where every one was fairly comfortable and fairly prosperous. You've always been a part of a community where people went to church and prayer-meeting and Sunday-school. Your neighbours loved each other, and played Pollyanna when things went wrong. And you wore white frocks and blue sashes whenever there was a lawn party or a sociable." He paused, perhaps for breath, and then - "I'm different," he said; "I struggled for my education; it was always the survival of the fittest with me. I worked my way through medical school. I had my hospital experience in Bellevue and on the Island - most of my patients were the lowest of the low. I've tried to cure diseased bodies - but I've left diseased minds alone. Diseased minds have been out of my line. Perhaps that's why I've come through with an ideal of life that's slightly different from your sunshine and apple blossoms theory!"

"Oh," Rose-Marie was half sobbing, "oh, you're so hard!"

The Young Doctor faced her suddenly and squarely. "Why did you come here," he cried, "to the slums? Why did you come to work in a Settlement House? What qualifications have you to be a social service worker, you child? What do you know of the meaning of service, of life?"

Rose-Marie's voice was earnest, though shaken.

"I came," she answered, "because I love people and want to help them. I came because I want to teach them to think beautiful thoughts, to have beautiful ideals. I came because I want to show them the God that I know - and try to serve -" she faltered.

The Young Doctor laughed - but not pleasantly.

"And I," he said, "came to make their bodies as healthy as possible. I came because curing sick bodies was my job - *not because I loved people or had any particular faith in them.* Prescribing to criminals and near-criminals isn't a reassuring work; it doesn't give one faith in human nature or in human souls!"

The Superintendent had been forgotten. But her tired voice rose suddenly across the barrier of speech that had grown high and icy between the Young Doctor and Rose-Marie.

"You both came," she said, and she spoke in the tone of a mother of chickens who has found two young and precocious ducklings in her brood, "you both came to help people - of that I'm sure!"

Rose-Marie started up, suddenly, from the table.

"I came," she said, as she moved toward the door that led to the hall, "to make people better."

"And I," said the Young Doctor, moving away from the table toward the opposite side of the room and another door, "I came to make them healthier!" With his hand on the knob of the door he spoke to the Superintendent.

"I'll not be back for supper," he said shortly, "I'll be too busy. Giovanni Celleni is out of jail again, and he's thrown his wife down a flight of stairs. She'll probably not live. And while Minnie Cohen was at the vaudeville show last night - developing her soul, perhaps - her youngest baby fell against the stove. Well, it'll be better for the baby if it does die! And there are others - " The door slammed upon his angry back.

Rose-Marie's face was white as she leaned against the dark wainscoting.

"Minnie Cohen brought the baby in last week," she shuddered, "such a dear baby! And Mrs. Celleni - she tried so hard! Oh, it's not right -" She was crying, rather wildly, as she went out of the room.

The Superintendent, left alone at the table, rang for the stolid maid. Her voice was carefully calm as she gave orders for the evening meal. If she was thinking of Giovanni Celleni, his brute face filled with semi-madness; if she was thinking of a burned baby, sobbing alone in a darkened tenement while its mother breathlessly watched the gay colours and shifting scenes of a make-believe life, her expression did not mirror her thought. Only once she spoke, as she was folding her napkin, and then -

"They're both very young," she murmured, a shade regretfully. Perhaps she was remembering the enthusiasm - and the intolerance - of her own youth.

III

CONCERNING IDEALS

"Sunshine and apple blossoms!" Rose-Marie, hurrying along the hall to her own room, repeated the Young Doctor's words and sobbed afresh as she repeated them. She tried to tell herself that nothing he could think mattered much to her, but there was a certain element of truth in everything that he had said. It was a fact that her life had been an unclouded, peaceful one - her days had followed each other as regularly, as innocuously, as blue china beads, strung upon a white cord, follow each other.

Of course, she told herself, she had never known a mother; and her father had died when she was a tiny girl. But she was forced to admit - as she had been forced to admit many times - that she did not particularly feel the lack of parents. Her two aunts, that she had always lived with, had been everything to her - they had indulged her, had made her pretty frocks, had never tried, in any way, to block the reachings of her personality. When she had decided suddenly, fired by the convincing address of a visiting city missionary, to leave the small town of her birth, they had put no obstacle in her path.

"If you feel that you must go," they had told her, "you

must. Maybe it is the work that the Lord has chosen for you. We have all faith in you, Rose-Marie!"

And Rose-Marie, splendid in her youth and assurance, had never known that their pillows were damp that night - and for many another night - with the tears that they were too brave to let her see.

They had packed her trunk, folding the white dress and the blue sash - Rose-Marie wondered how the Young Doctor had known about the dress and sash - in tissue paper. They had created a blue serge frock for work, and a staunch little blue coat, and a blue tam-o'-shanter. Rose-Marie would have been aghast to know how childish she looked in that tam-o'-shanter! Her every-day shoes had been resoled; her white ruffled petticoats had been lengthened. And then she had been launched, like a slim little boat, upon the turbulent sea of the city!

Looking back, through a mist of angry tears, Rose-Marie felt her first moment of homesickness for the friendly little town with its wide, tree-shaded streets, its lawn parties, and its neighbours; cities, she had discovered, discourage the art of neighbouring! She felt a pang of emptiness - she wanted her aunts with their soft, interested eyes, and their tender hands.

At first the city had thrilled her. But now that she had been in the Settlement House a month, the thrill was beginning to die away. The great buildings were still unbelievably high, the crowds of people were still a strange and mysterious throng, the streets were as colourful as ever - but life, nevertheless, was beginning to settle into ordinary channels.

She had thought, at the beginning of her stay there, that the Settlement House was a hotbed of romance. Every ring of the doorbell had tingled through her; every step in the hall had made her heart leap, with a strange quickening movement, into her throat - every shabby man had been to her a possible tragedy, every thread-bare woman had been a case for charity. She had fluttered from reception-hall to reading-room, and back again - she had been alert, breathless, eager.

But, with the assignment of regular duties, some of the adventure had been drained from life. For her these consisted of teaching a club of girls to sew, of instructing a group of mothers in the art of making cakes and pies and salads, and of hearing a half hundred little children repeat their A B Cs. Only the difference in setting, only the twang of foreign tongues, only the strange precociousness of the children, made life at all different from the life at home. She told herself, fiercely, that she might be a teacher in a district school - a country school - for all the good she was accomplishing.

She had offered, so many times, to do visiting in the tenements - to call upon families of the folk who would not come to the Settlement House. But the Superintendent had met her, always, with a denial that was wearily firm.

"I have a staff of women - older women from outside - who do the visiting," she had said. "I'm afraid" she was eyeing Rose-Marie in the blue coat and the blue tam-o'-shanter, "I'm afraid that you'd scarcely be - convincing. And," she had added, "Dr. Blanchard takes care of all the detail in that department of our work!"

Dr. Blanchard ... Rose-Marie felt the tears coming afresh at the thought of him! She remembered how she had written home enthusiastic, schoolgirlish letters about the handsome man who sat across the dining table from her. It had seemed exciting, romantic, that only the three of them really should live in the great brownstone house - the Young Doctor, the Superintendent - who made a perfect chaperon - and herself. It had seemed, somehow, almost providential that they should be thrown together. Yes, Rose-Marie remembered how she had been attracted to Dr. Blanchard at the very first - how she had found nothing wanting in his wiry strength, his broad shoulders, his dark, direct eyes.

But she had not been in the Settlement House long before she began to feel the clash of their natures. When she started to church service, on her first Sunday in New York, she surprised a smile of something that might have been cynical mirth upon his lean, square-jawed face. And when she spoke of the daily prayers that she and her aunts had so beautifully believed in, back in the little town, he laughed at her - not unkindly, but with the sympathetic superiority that one feels for a too trusting child. Rose-Marie, thinking it over, knew that she would rather meet direct unkindness than that bland superiority!

And so - though there had never been an open quarrel until the one at the luncheon table - Rose-Marie had learned to look to the Superintendent for encouragement, rather than to the Young Doctor. And she had frigidly declined his small courtesies - a visit to the movies, a walk in the park, a 'bus ride up Fifth Avenue.

"I never went to the movies at home," she had told

Margaret E. Sangster

him. Or, "I'm too busy, just now, to take a walk." Or, "I can't go with you to-day. I've letters to write."

"It's a shame," she confided, on occasion, to the Superintendent, "that Dr. Blanchard never goes to church. It's a shame that he has had so little religious life. I gave him a book to read the other day - the letters of an American Missionary in China - and he laughed and told me that he couldn't waste his time. What do you think of that! But later," Rose-Marie's voice sank to a horrified whisper, "later, I saw him reading a cheap novel - he had time for a cheap novel!"

The Superintendent looked down into Rose-Marie's earnest little face.

"My dear," she said gently, stifling a desire to laugh, "my dear, he's a very busy man. He gives a great deal of himself to the people here in the slums. The novel, to him, was just a mental relaxation."

But to the Young Doctor, later, the Superintendent spoke differently.

"Billy Blanchard," she said, and she only called him Billy Blanchard when she wanted to scold him, "I've known you for a long time. And I'm sure that there's no harm in you. Of course," she sighed, "I wish that you could feel a little more in sympathy with the spiritual side of our work. But I've argued with you, more than once, on that point!"

The doctor, who was packing medicines into his bag, looked up.

"You know, you old dear," he told her, "that I'm

hopeless. I haven't had an easy row to hoe, not ever; you wouldn't be religious yourself if you were in my shoes! There - don't look so shocked - you've been a mother to me in your funny, fussy way, since I came to this place! That's the main reason, I guess, that I stick here, as I do, when I could make a lot more money somewhere else!" He reached up to pat her thin hand, and then, "But why are you worrying, just now, about my soul?" he questioned.

The Superintendent sighed again.

"It's the little Thompson girl," she answered; "she's so anxious to convert people, and she's so sincere, - so very sincere. I can't help feeling that you are a thorn in her flesh, Billy. She says that you won't read her missionary books -"

The Young Doctor interrupted.

"She's such a pretty girl," he said quite fiercely. "Why on earth didn't she stay at home, where she belonged! Why on earth did she pick out this sort of work?"

The Superintendent answered.

"One never knows," she said, "why girls pick out certain kinds of work. I've had the strangest cases come to my office - of homely girls who wanted to be artists' models, and anemic girls who wanted to be physical directors, and flighty girls who wanted to go to Bible School, and quiet girls who were all set for a career on the stage. Rose-Marie Thompson is the sort of a girl who was cut out to be a home-maker, to give happiness to some nice, clean boy, to have a nursery full of rosy-cheeked babies. And yet here she is, filled with a desire to rescue people, to snatch brands from the burning. Here she is in the slums when she'd be dramatically right in an apple orchard - at the time of year when the trees are covered with pink and white blossoms."

The Young Doctor laughed. He so well understood the Superintendent - so enjoyed her point of view.

"Yes," he agreed, "she'd be perfect there in an organdy frock with the sun slanting across her face. But - well, she's just like other girls. Tell a pretty girl that she's clever, they say, and tell a clever girl that she's a raving, tearing beauty. That's the way for a man to be popular!"

The Superintendent laughed quietly with him. It was a moment before she grew sober again.

"I wonder," she said at last, "why you have never tried to be popular with girls. You could so easily be popular. You're young and - don't try to hush me up - good-looking. And yet - well, you're such an antagonistic person. From the very first you've laughed at Rose-Marie - and she was quite ready to adore you when she arrived. How do I know? Oh, I could tell! Take the child seriously, Billy Blanchard, before she actually begins to dislike you!"

The Young Doctor put several bottles of violently coloured pills into his bag before he spoke.

"She dislikes me already," he said. "She's such a cool little person. What are you trying to do, anyway? Are you trying to matchmake; to stir up a love affair between the both of us -" suddenly he was laughing again.

"I'm too busy to have a romance, you old dear," he told the Superintendent, "far too busy. I'm as likely to fall in love, just now, as you are!"

The woman's face was averted as she answered. But her low voice was steady.

"When I was your age, Billy," she said gently, "I *was* in love. That's why, perhaps, I came here. That's why, perhaps, I stayed. No, he didn't die - he married another girl. And dreams are hard things to forget. That's why I left the country. Maybe that's why the little Thompson girl - "

But the Young Doctor was shaking his head.

"She hasn't had any love affair," he told the Superintendent. "She's too young and full of ideals to have anything so ordinary as a romance. Everybody," his laugh was not too pleasant, "can have a romance! And few people can be so filled with ideals as Miss Thompson. Oh, it's her ideals that I can't stand! It's her impractical way of gazing at life through pink-coloured glasses. She'll never be of any real use here in the slums. I'm only afraid that she'll come to some harm because she's so trusting and over-sincere. I'd hate to see her placed in direct contact with some of the young men that I work with, for instance. You haven't - " All at once his voice took on a new note. "You haven't let her be with any of the boys' classes, have you? Her ideals might not stand the strain!"

The Superintendent answered.

"Ideals don't hurt any one," she said, and her voice was almost as fierce as the doctor's. "No, I haven't given her a bit of work with the boys. She's too young and too untouched and, as you say, too pretty. I'm letting her spend her time with the mothers, and the young girls, and the little tots - not even allowing her to go out alone, if I can help it. Such innocence - " The Superintendent broke off suddenly in the middle of the sentence. And she sighed again.

IV

THE PARK

Crying helps, sometimes. When Rose-Marie, alone in her room, finally dried away the tears that were the direct result of her quarrel with Dr. Blanchard, there was a new resolve in her eyes - a look that had not been there when she went, an hour before, to the luncheon table. It was the look of one who has resolutions that cannot be shattered - dreams that are unbreakable. She glanced at her wrist watch and there was a shade of defiance in the very way she raised the arm that wore it.

"They make a baby of me here," she told herself, "they treat me like a silly child. It's a wonder that they don't send a nurse-maid with me to my classes. It's a wonder" - she was growing vehement - "that they give me credit for enough sense to wear rubbers when it's raining! I," again she glanced at the watch, "I haven't a single thing to do until four o'clock - and it's only just a little after two. I'm going out - *now*. I'm going into the streets, or into a tenement, or into a - a *dive*, if necessary! I'm going to show them" - the plural pronoun, strangely, referred to a certain young man - "that I can help somebody! I'm going to show them -"

She was struggling eagerly into her coat; eagerly she

pulled her tam-o'-shanter over the curls that, even in the city slums, were full of sunshine. With her hands thrust staunchly into her pockets, she went out; out into the jungle of streets that met, as in the center of a labyrinth, in front of the Settlement House.

Always, when she had gone out alone, she had sought a small park not far from her new home. It was a comfortingly green little oasis in the desert of stone and brick - a little oasis that reminded one of the country. She turned toward it now, quite blindly, for the streets confused her - they always did. As the crowds closed around her she hurried vaguely, as a swimmer hurries just before he loses his head and goes down. She caught her breath as she went, for the crowds always made her feel submerged - quite as the swimmer feels just before the final plunge. She entered the park - it was scarcely more than a square of grass - with a very definite feeling of relief, almost of rescue.

As usual, the park was crowded. But park crowds are different from street crowds - they are crowds at rest, rather than hurrying, restless throngs. Rose-Marie sank upon an iron bench and with wide, childishly distended eyes surveyed the people that surged in upon her.

There was a woman with a hideous black wig - the badge of revered Jewish motherhood - pressed down over the front of her silvered hair. Rose-Marie, a short time ago, would have guessed her age at seventy - now she told herself that the woman was probably forty. There was a slim, cigarette-smoking youth with pale, shifty eyes. There was an old, old man - white-bearded like one of the patriarchs - and there was a dark-browed girl who held a drowsy baby to her breast. All of these and many more - Italians, Slavs, Russians,

Hungarians and an occasional Chinaman - passed her by. It seemed to the girl that this section was a veritable melting pot of the races - and that every example of every race was true to type. She had seen any number of young men with shifty eyes - she had seen many old men with white beards. She knew that other black-wigged women lived in every tenement; that other dark-browed girls were, at that same moment, rocking other babies. She fell to wondering, whimsically, whether God had fashioned the people of the slums after some half-dozen set patterns - almost as the cutter, in many an alley sweatshop, fashions the frocks of a season.

A sharp cry broke in upon her wonderings. It was the cry of an animal in utter pain - in blind, unreasoning agony. Rose-Marie was on her feet at the first moment that it cut, quiveringly, through the air. With eyes distended she whirled about to face a small boy who knelt upon the ground behind her bench.

To Rose-Marie the details of the small boy's appearance came back, later, with an amazing clarity. Later she could have described his dark, sullen eyes, his mouth with its curiously grim quirk at one corner, his shock of black hair and his ragged coat. But at the moment she had the ability to see only one thing - the scrawny gray kitten that the boy had tied to the iron leg of the bench; the shrinking kitten that the boy was torturing with a cold, relentless cruelty.

It shrieked again - with an almost human cry - as she started around the bench toward it. And the wild throbbing of her heart told her that she was witnessing, for the first time, a phase of human nature of which she had never dreamed.

V

ROSE-MARIE COMES TO THE RESCUE

Rose-Marie's hand upon the small boy's coat collar was not gentle. With surprising strength, for she was small and slight, she jerked him aside.

"You wicked child!" she exclaimed, and the Young Doctor would have chuckled to hear her tone. "You wicked child, what are you doing?"

Without waiting for an answer she knelt beside the pitiful little animal that was tied to the bench, and with trembling fingers unloosed the cord that held it, noting as she did so how its bones showed, even through its coat of fur. When it was at liberty she gathered it close to her breast and turned to face the boy.

He had not tried to run away. Even with the anger surging through her, Rose-Marie admitted that the child was not - in one sense - a coward. He had waited, brazenly perhaps, to hear what she had to say. With blazing eyes she said it:

"Why," she questioned, and the anger that made her eyes blaze also put a tremor into her voice, "why were you deliberately hurting this kitten? Don't you know that kittens can feel pain just as much as you can feel pain? Don't you know that it is wicked to make anything suffer? Why were you so wicked?"

The boy looked up at her with sullen, dark eyes. The grim twist at one corner of his mouth became more pronounced.

"Aw," he said gruffly, "why don't yer mind yer own business?"

If Rose-Marie's hands had been free, she would have taken the boy suddenly and firmly by both shoulders. She felt an overwhelming desire to shake him - to shake him until his teeth chattered. But both of her hands were busy, soothing the gray kitten that shivered against her breast.

"I am minding my own business," she told the boy. "It's my business to give help where it's needed, and this kitten," she cuddled it closer, "certainly needed help! Haven't you ever been told that you should be kind? Like," she faltered, "like Jesus was kind? He wouldn't have hurt anything. He loved animals - and He loved boys, too. Why don't you try to be the sort of a boy He could love? Why do you try to be bad - to do wrong things?"

The eyes of the child were even more sullen - the twist of his mouth was even more grim as he listened to Rose-Marie. But when she had finished speaking, he answered her - and still he did not try to run away.

"Wot," he questioned, almost in the words of the Young Doctor, "wot do you know about things that's right an' things that's wrong? It ain't bad t' hurt animals - not if they're little enough so as they ain't able t' hurt you!"

Rose-Marie sat down, very suddenly, upon the bench. In all of her life - her sheltered, glad life - she had never heard such a brutal creed spoken, and from the lips of a child! Her eyes, searching his face, saw that he was not trying to be funny, or saucy, or smart. Curiously enough she noted that he was quite sincere - that, to him, the torturing of a kitten was only a part of the day with its various struggles and amusements. When she spoke again her tone was gentle - as gentle as the tone with which the other slum children, who came to the Settlement House, were familiar.

"Whoever told you," she questioned, "that it's not wrong to hurt an animal, so long as it can't fight back?"

The boy eyed her strangely. Rose-Marie could almost detect a gleam of latent interest in his dark eyes. And then, as if he had gained a sort of confidence in her, he answered.

"Nobody never told me," he said gruffly. "But I *know*."

The kitten against Rose-Marie's breast cried piteously. Perhaps it was the hopelessness of the cry that made her want so desperately to make the boy understand. Conquering the loathing she had felt toward him she managed the ghost of a smile.

"I wish," she said, and the smile became firmer, brighter, as she said it, "I wish that you'd sit down, here, beside me. I want to tell you about the animals that I've had for pets - and about how they loved me. I had a white dog once; his name was Dick. He used to go to the store for me, he used to carry my bundles home in his mouth - and he did tricks -"

The boy had seated himself, gingerly, on the bench. He interrupted her, and his voice was eager.

"Did yer have t' beat him," he questioned, "t' make him do the tricks? Did he bleed when yer beat him?"

Again Rose-Marie gasped. She leaned forward until her face was on a level with the boy's face.

"Why," she asked him, "do you think that the only way to teach an animal is to teach him by cruelty? I taught my dog tricks by being kind and sweet to him. Why do you talk of beatings - I couldn't hurt anything, even if I disliked it, until it *bled*!"

The small boy drew back from Rose-Marie. His expression was vaguely puzzled - it seemed almost as if he did not comprehend what her words meant.

"My pa beats me," he said suddenly, "always he beats me - when he's drunk! An' sometimes he beats me when he ain't. He beats Ma, too, an' he uster beat Jim, 'n' Ella. He don't dare beat Jim now, though" - this proudly - "Jim's as big as he is now, an' Ella - nobody'd dast lay a hand on Ella ..." almost as suddenly as he had started to talk, the boy stopped.

For the moment the episode of the kitten was a forgotten thing. There was only pity, only a blank sort of horror, on Rose-Marie's face.

"Doesn't your father love you - any of you?" she asked.

"Naw." The boy's mouth was a straight line - a straight

and very bitter line, for such a young mouth. "Naw, he only loves his booze. He hits me all th' time - an' he's four times as big as me! An' so I hit whoever's smaller'n I am. An' even if they cry I don't care. I hate things that's little - that can't take care o' themselves. Everything had oughter be able t' take care of itself!"

"Haven't you" - again Rose-Marie asked a question - "haven't you ever loved anything that was smaller than you are? Haven't you ever had a pet? Haven't you ever felt that you must protect and take care of some one - or something? Haven't you?"

All at once the boy was smiling, and the smile lit up his small, dark face as a candle, slowly flickering, brings cheer and brightness to a dull, lonely room.

"I love Lily," he told her. "I wouldn't let nobody touch Lily! If Pa so much as spoke mean to her - I'd kill him. I'd kill him with a knife!"

Rose-Marie shuddered inwardly at the thought. But her voice was very even as she spoke.

"Who is Lily?" she asked.

The boy had slid down along the bench. He was so close to her that his shabby coat sleeve touched her blue one.

"Lily's my kid sister," he said, and, miracle of miracles, his voice held a note of tenderness. "Say - Miss, I'm sorry I hurt th' cat."

With a sudden feeling of warmth Rose-Marie moved just a fraction of an inch closer to the boy. She knew, somehow, that his small, curiously abject apology was in a way related to the "kid sister"; she knew, almost instinctively, that this Lily who could make a smile come to the dark little face, who could make a tenderness dwell in those hard young eyes, was the only avenue by which she could reach this strange child. She spoke to him suddenly, impulsively.

"I'd like to see your Lily; I'd like to see her, awfully," she told him. "Will you bring her some time to call on me? I live at the Settlement House."

A subtle change had come over the child's face. He slid, hurriedly, from the bench.

"Oh," he said, "yer one o' them! You sing hymns 'n' pray 'n' tell folks t' take baths. I know. Well, I can't bring Lily t' see you - not ever!"

Rose-Marie had also risen to her feet.

"Then," she said eagerly, "let me come and see Lily. Where do you live?"

The boy's eyes had fallen. It was plain that he did not want to answer - that he was experiencing the almost inarticulate embarrassment of childhood.

"We live," he told her at last, "in that house over there." His pointing finger indicated the largest and grimiest of the tenements that loomed, dark and high, above the squalor of a side street. "But you wouldn't wanter come - there!"

Rose-Marie caught her breath sharply. She was remembering how the Superintendent had forbidden her to do visiting, how the Young Doctor had laughed at her desire to be of service. She knew what they would say if she told them that she was going into a tenement to see a strange child named Lily. Perhaps that was why her voice had an excited ring as she answered.

"Yes, I would come there!" she told the boy. "Tell me what floor you live on, and what your name is, and when it would be best for me to come?"

"My name's Bennie Volsky," the boy said slowly. "We're up five flights, in th' back. D'yer really mean that you'll come - an' see Lily?"

Rose-Marie nodded soberly. How could the child know that her heart was all athrob with the call of a great adventure?

"Yes, I mean it," she told him. "When shall I come?"

The boy's grubby hand shot out and rested upon her sleeve.

"Come to-morrow afternoon," he told her. "Say, yer all right!" He turned, swiftly, and ran through the crowd, and in a moment had disappeared like a small drab-coloured city chameleon.

Rose-Marie, standing by the bench, watched the place where he had disappeared. And then, all at once, she turned swiftly - just as swiftly as the boy had - and started back across the park toward the Settlement House.

"I won't tell them!" she was saying over and over in

her heart, as she went, "I won't tell them! They wouldn't let me go, if I did.... I won't tell them!"

The kitten was still held tight in her arms. It rested, quite contentedly, against her blue coat. Perhaps it knew that there was a warm, friendly place - even for little frightened animals - in the Settlement House.

VI

"THERE'S NO PLACE -"

When Rose-Marie paused in front of the tenement, at three o'clock on the following afternoon, she felt like a naughty little girl who is playing truant from school. When she remembered the way that she had avoided the Superintendent's almost direct questions, she blushed with an inward sense of shame. But when she thought of the Young Doctor's offer to go with her - "wherever she was going" - she threw back her head with a defiant little gesture. She knew well that the Young Doctor was sorry for yesterday's quarrel - she knew that a night beside the dying Mrs. Celleni, and the wails of the Cohen baby, had temporarily softened his viewpoint upon life. And yet - he had said that they were soulless - these people that she had come to help! He would have condemned Bennie Volsky from the first - but she had detected the glimmerings of something fine in the child! No - despite his more tolerant attitude - she knew that, underneath, his convictions were unchanged. She was glad that she had gone out upon her adventure alone.

With a heart that throbbed in quick staccato beats, she mounted the steps of the tenement. Little dark-eyed children moved away from her, apparently on every side, but somehow she scarcely noticed them. The doorway yawned, like an open mouth, in front of her - and she could think of nothing else. As she went over the dark threshold she remembered stories that she had read about people who go in at tenement doorways and are never seen again. Every one has read such stories in the daily newspapers - and perhaps some of them are true!

A faint light flickered in through the doorway. It made the ascent of the first flight of creaking stairs quite easy. At least Rose-Marie could step aside from the piles of rubbish and avoid the rickety places. She wondered, as she went up, her fingers gingerly touching the dirty hand-rail, how people could exist under such wretched conditions.

The second flight was harder to manage. The light from the narrow doorway was shut off, and there were no windows. There might have been gas jets upon every landing - Rose-Marie supposed that there were - but it was mid-afternoon, and they had not yet been lighted. She groped her way up the second flight, and the third, feeling carefully along each step with her foot before she put her weight upon it.

On the fourth flight she paused for a moment to catch her breath. But she realized, as she paused, that even breathing had to be done under difficulties in this place. There was no ventilation of any sort, so far as she could tell - all about her floated the odours of boiled cabbage, and fried onions, and garlic. And there were other odours, too; the indescribable smells of soiled clothing and soap-suds and greasy dishes.

But in Rose-Marie's mind, the odours - poignant though they were - took second place to the sounds.

Never, she told herself, had she imagined that so many different sorts of noises could exist in the same place at one and the same time. There were the cries and sobs of little children, the moans of sickness, the thuds of falling furniture and the crashes of breaking crockery. There were yells of rage, and - worst of all - bursts of appalling profanity. Rose-Marie, standing there in the darkness of the fourth flight, heard words that she had never expected to hear - phrases of which she had never dreamed. She shuddered as she started up the fifth flight, and when, at last, she stood in front of the Volsky flat, she experienced almost a feeling of relief. At least she would be shut off, in a moment, from those alien and terrible sounds - at least, in a moment, she would be in a *home*.

To most of us - particularly if we have grown up in an atmosphere such as had always sheltered Rose-Marie - the very sound of the word "home" brings a certain sense of warmth and comfort. Home stands for shelter and protection and love. "Be it ever so humble," the old song tells us, "be it ever so humble ..."

And Rose-Marie, knocking timidly upon the Volsky door, expected to find a home. She expected it to be humble in the truest sense of the word - to be ragged and poverty-stricken and mean. And yet she could not feel that it would be utterly divorced from the ideals she had always built around her conception of the word. She expected it to be a home because a family lived there together - a mother, and a father, and children.

In answer to her knock the door swung open - a little way. The glow of a dingy lamp fell about her, through the opening - she felt suddenly as if she had been swept, willy-nilly, before the footlights of some hostile stage. For a moment she stood blinking. And as she stood there, quite unable to see, she heard the voice of Bennie Volsky, speaking in a hoarse whisper.

"It's you, Miss!" said the voice, and it was as full of intense wonderment as a voice could be. "I never thought that you'd come - I didn't think you was on th' level. So many folks say they'll do things -" he broke off, and then - "Walk in, quiet," he told her slowly. "Don't make any noise, if yer can help it! Pa's come home, all lit up. An' he's asleep, in th' corner! There'll be - " he broke off - "There'll be th' dickens t' pay, if Pa wakes up! But walk in, still-like. An' yer can see Ma an' all, an' - *Lily*!"

Rose-Marie, whose eyes had now become accustomed to the dim light, stepped past the boy and into the room. Her hand, in passing, touched his arm lightly, for she knew that he was labouring under intense excitement. She stepped into the room, on mousy-quiet feet - and then, with a quick gasp, drew back again.

Never, in her wildest dreams of poverty, had Rose-Marie supposed that squalor, such as she saw in the Volsky home, could exist. Never had she supposed that a family could live in such cramped, airless quarters. Never had she thought that filth, such as she saw in the room, was possible. It all seemed, somehow, an unbelievably bad dream - a dream in which she was appearing, with startling realism. Her comfortable picture of a home was vanishing - vanishing as suddenly and completely as a soap bubble vanishes, if pricked by a pin.

"Why - why, Bennie!" she began. But the child was

Margaret E. Sangster

not listening. He had darted from her side and was dragging forward, by one listless, work-coarsened hand, a pallid, drooping woman.

"Dis is my ma," he told Rose-Marie. "She didn't know yer was comin'. I didn't tell her!"

It seemed to Rose-Marie that there was a scared sort of appeal in the woman's eyes as they travelled, slowly, over her face. But there was not even appeal in the tone of her voice - it was all a drab, colourless monotone.

"Whatcha come here fer?" she questioned. "Pa, he's home. If he should ter wake up - " She left the sentence unfinished.

Almost instinctively the eyes of Rose-Marie travelled past the figure of Mrs. Volsky. There was nothing in that figure to hold her gaze - it was so vague, so like a shadow of something that had been. She saw the few broken chairs, the half-filled wash tub, the dish-pan with its freight of soiled cups and plates. She saw the gas stove, with its battered coffee-pot, and a mattress or two piled high with dingy bedding. And, in one corner, she saw - with a new sense of horror - the reclining figure of Pa.

Pa was sleeping. Sleeping heavily, with his mouth open and his tousled head slipping to one side. One great hairy hand was clenched about an empty bottle - one huge foot, stockingless and half out of its shoe, was dragging limply off the heap of blankets that was his bed. A stubble of beard made his already dark face even more sinister, his tousled hair looked as if it had never known the refining influences of a comb or brush. As Rose-Marie stared at him, half fascinated, he turned - with a spasmodic, drunken movement - and flung one heavy arm above his head.

The room was not a large one. But, at that moment, it seemed appallingly spacious to Rose-Marie. She turned, almost with a feeling of affection, toward Bennie. At least she had seen him before. And, as if he interpreted her feeling, Bennie spoke.

"We got two other rooms," he told her, "one that Ella an' Lily sleep in, an' one that Jim pays fer, his own self. Ma an' Pa an' me - we sleep *here*! Say, don't you be too scared o' Pa - he'll stay asleep fer a long time, now. He won't wake up unless he's shook. Will he, Ma?"

Mrs. Volsky nodded her head with a worn out, apathetic movement. Noiselessly, but with the appearance of a certain terrible effort under the shell of quiet, she moved away across the room toward the stove.

"She's goin' t' warm up th' coffee," Bennie said. "She'll give you some, in a minute, if yer want it!"

Rose-Marie was about to speak, about to assure Bennie that she didn't want any of the coffee, when steps sounded on the stairs. They were hurried steps; steps suggesting to the listener that five flights were nothing, after all! Rose-Marie found herself turning as a hand fell heavily upon a door-knob, and the door swung in.

A young man stood jauntily upon the threshold. Rose-Marie's first impression of him was one of extreme, almost offensive neatness - of sleek hair, that looked like patent leather, and of highly polished brown shoes.

She saw that his blue and white striped collar was speckless, that his blue tie was obviously new, that his trousers were creased to an almost dangerous edge. But it was the face of the young man from which Rose-Marie shrank back - a clever, sharp face with narrow, horribly speculative eyes and a thin-lipped red mouth. It was a handsome face, yes, but -

The voice of Bennie broke, suddenly, across her speculations. "Jim," he said.

Still jauntily - Rose-Marie realized that jauntiness was his keynote - the young man entered the room. His sharp eyes travelled with lightning-like rapidity over the place, resting a moment on the sleeping figure of Pa before they hurried past him to Rose-Marie. He surveyed her coolly, taking in every feature, every fold of her garments, with a studied boldness that was somehow offensive.

"Who's she?" he questioned abruptly, of any one who cared to answer, and one manicured finger pointed in her direction. "Where'd she come from?"

Bennie was the one who spoke. Rather gallantly he stepped in front of Rose-Marie.

"She's a friend of mine," he said; "she lives by th' Settlement House. She come up here t' see me, 'n' Ma, 'n' Lily. You leave her be - y' understand?"

The young man laughed, and his laugh was curiously hard and dry.

"Oh, sure!" he told Bennie. "I'll leave her be! What," he turned to Rose-Marie with an insolent smile, "what's yer name?"

Rose-Marie met his insolent gaze with a calm expression. No one would have guessed that she was trembling inwardly.

"My name," she told him, "is Rose-Marie Thompson. I live in the Settlement House, and I came to see your sister."

"Well," the young man's insolent gaze was still studying Rose-Marie, "well, she'll be up soon. I passed 'er on th' stairs. But," he laughed again, "why didn't yer come t' see me - huh?"

Rose-Marie, having no answer, turned expectantly toward the door. If this Jim had passed his sister on the stairs, she couldn't be very far away. As if in reply to her supposition, the door swung open again and a tall, dark-eyed girl came into the room. Rose-Marie saw with her first swift glance that the red upon the girl's cheeks was too high to be quite natural - that the scarlet of her lips was over-vivid. And yet, despite the patently artificial colouring, she realized that the girl was beautiful with a high strung, almost thoroughbred beauty. She wondered how this beauty had been born of the dim woman who seemed so colourless and the sodden brute who lay snoring in the comer.

Her train of thought was broken, suddenly. For the young man was speaking. Rose-Marie disliked, some-how, the very tone of his voice.

"Here's a girl t' see you, Ella," he said. "She's from th' Settlement House - she says! Maybe she wants," sarcastically, "that you should join a Bible Class!"

The girl's eyes were flashing with a dangerously hard light. She turned angrily to Rose-Marie. But before she could say anything, the child, Bennie, had interposed.

"She didn't come t' see *you*" he told his older sister - "she don't want t' see you - like those other wimmen did. She come t' see *Lily* -"

He paused and Rose-Marie, who had gathered that social service workers were not welcome visitors, went on breathlessly, from where he left off.

"I *am* from the Settlement House," she told Ella, "and I'd like awfully to have you join our classes. But that wasn't why I came here. Bennie told me that he had a dear little sister. And I came to see her."

A change swept miraculously over Ella's cold face. Rose-Marie could see, all at once, that she and her young brother were strikingly alike - that Jim was the different one in this family.

"I'll get Lily," Ella said simply, and there was a warmth, a tenderness in her dark eyes that had been so hard. "I didn't understand," she added, as she went quickly past Rose-Marie and into the small inner room that Bennie had said his sisters shared. In a moment she came out leading a small girl by the hand.

"This is Lily!" she said softly.

Even in that dingy place - perhaps accentuated by the very dinginess of it - Lily's blond loveliness struck Rose-Marie with a sense of shock. The child might have been a flower - the very flower whose name she bore - growing upon an ash heap. Her beauty made the rest of the room fade into dim outlines - made Jim and Ella and Bennie seem heavy, and somehow overfed. Even Pa, snoring lustily, became almost a shadow. Rose-Marie stepped toward the child impulsively, with outflung arms.

"Oh, you dear!" she said shakily, "you dear!"

Nobody spoke. Only Ella, with gentle hands, pushed her little sister forward. The child's great blue eyes looked past Rose-Marie, and a vague smile quivered on her lips.

"Oh, you dear!" Rose-Marie exclaimed again, and went down on her knees on the dirty floor - real women will always kneel before a beautiful child.

Lily might have been four years old. Her hair, drawn back from her white little face, was the colour of pale gold, and her lips were faintly coral. But it was her deep eyes, with their vague expression, that clutched, somehow, at Rose-Marie's heart.

"Tell me that you're going to like me, Lily!" she almost implored. "I love little girls."

The child did not answer - indeed, she did not seem to hear. But one thin little hand, creeping out, touched Rose-Marie's face with a gesture that was singularly appealing, singularly full of affection. When the fingers touched her cheek, Rose-Marie felt a sudden suspicion, a sudden dread. She noticed, all at once, that no one was speaking - that the room was quite still, except for the beastial grunts of the sleeping Pa.

"Why," she asked, quite without meaning to, "why

Margaret E. Sangster

doesn't she answer me? She isn't afraid of me, is she? Why doesn't she say something?"

It was, curiously enough, Mrs. Volsky who answered. Even her voice - that was usually so dull and monotonous - held a certain tremor.

"Lily," she said slowly, "can't spick - 'r hear.... An' she's - blind!"

VII

A LILY IN THE SLUMS

Rose-Marie started back from the child with a sickening sense of shock. All at once she realized the reason why Bennie's eyes grew tender at the mention of his little sister - why Ella forgot anger and suspicion when Lily came into the room. She understood why Mrs. Volsky's dull voice held love and sorrow. And yet, as she looked at the small girl, it seemed almost incredible that she should be so afflicted. Deaf and dumb and blind! Never to hear the voices of those who loved her, never to see the beautiful things of life, never - even - to speak! Rose-Marie choked back a sob, and glanced across the child's cloud of pale golden hair at Ella. As their eyes met she knew that they were, in some strange way, friends.

With a sudden, overwhelming pity, her arms reached out again to Lily. As she gathered the child close she was surprised at the slenderness of the tiny figure, at the neatness of the faded gingham frock that blended in tone with the great, sightless eyes. All at once she remembered what Bennie had said to her, the day before, in the park.

"I love Lily," he had told her, "I wouldn't let nobody hurt Lily! If any one - even Pa, so much as spoke mean to her - I'd kill him...."

Glancing about the room, at the faces of the others, she sensed a silent echo of Bennie's words. Mrs. Volsky, who would keep neither her flat nor herself neat, quite evidently saw to it that Lily's little dress was spotless. Ella, whose temper would flare up at the slightest word, cared for the child with the tender efficiency of a professional nurse; Bennie's face, as he looked at his tiny sister, had taken on a cherubic softness. And Jim ... Rose-Marie glanced at Jim and was startled out of her reflections. For Jim was not looking at Lily. His gaze was fixed upon her own face with an intensity that frightened her. With a sudden impulse she spoke directly to him.

"You must be very kind to this little sister of yours," she told him. "She needs every bit of love and affection and consideration that her family can give her!"

Jim, his gaze still upon her face, shrugged his shoulders. But before he could answer Ella had come a step closer to Rose-Marie. Her eyes were flashing.

"Jim," she said, "ain't got any love or kindness or consideration in him! Jim thinks that Lily ain't got any more feelin's than a puppy dog - 'cause she can't answer back. Oh," in response to the question in Rose-Marie's face, "oh, he'd never put a finger on her - not that! But he don't speak kind to her, like we do. It's enough fer him that she can't hear th' words he lays his tongue to. Even Pa -"

Suddenly, as if in answer to his spoken name, there came a scuffling sound from the corner where Pa was sleeping. All at once the empty bottle dropped from the unclenched hand, the mouth fell open in a prodigious yawn, the eyes became wide, burned-out wells of drunkenness. And as she watched, Rose-Marie saw the room cleared in an amazing fashion. She heard Mrs. Volsky's terrified whisper, "He's wakin' up!" She heard Jim's harsh laugh; she saw Ella, with a fiercely maternal sweep of her strong arms, gather the little Lily close to her breast and dart toward the inner room. And then, as she stood dazedly watching the mountain of sodden flesh that was Pa rear itself to a sitting posture, and then to a standing one, she felt a hot little hand touch her own.

"We better clear out," said the voice of Bennie. "We better clear out pretty quick! Pa's awful bad, sometimes, when he's just wakin' up!"

With a quickness not unlike the bump at the end of a falling-through-space dream, Rose-Marie felt herself drawn from the room - heard the door close with a slam behind her. And then she was hurrying after the shadowy form of Bennie, down the five rickety flights of stairs - past the same varied odours and the same appalling sounds that she had noticed on the way up!

VIII

ANOTHER QUARREL

When Rose-Marie came out into the sunlight of the street she glanced at her watch and saw, with an almost overwhelming surprise, that it was only four o'clock. It was just an hour since she had entered the cavern-like doorway of the tenement. But in that hour she had come, for the first time, against life in the rough. She had seen degeneracy, and poverty, and - she was thinking of the expression in Jim's eyes - a menace that she did not at all understand. She had seen the waste of broken middle age and the pity of blighted childhood. She had seen fear and, if she had stayed a few moments longer, she would have seen downright brutality. Her hand, reaching out, clutched Bennie's hand.

"Dear," she said - and realized, from the startled expression of his eyes, that he had not often been called "Dear," - "is it always like that, in your home?"

Bennie looked up into her eyes. He seemed, somehow, younger than he had appeared the day before, younger and softer.

"Yes, Miss," he told her, "it's always like that, except when it's worse!"

"And," Rose-Marie was still asking questions, "do your older sister and brother just drift in, at any time, like that? And is your father home in the middle of the day? Don't any of them work?"

Bennie's barriers of shyness had been burned away by the warmth of her friendship. He was in a mood to tell anything.

"Pa, he works sometimes," he said. "An' Ella - she uster work till she had a fight with her boss last week. An' now she says she ain't gotta work no more 'cause there's a feller as will give her everythin' she wants, if she says th' word! An' Jim - I ain't never seen him do nothin', but he always has a awful lot o' money. He must do his workin' at night - after I'm asleep!"

Rose-Marie, her mind working rapidly, realized that Bennie had given revelations of which he did not even dream. Pa - his condition was what she had supposed it to be - but Ella was drifting toward danger-shoals that she had never imagined! Well she knew the conditions under which a girl of Ella's financial status stops working - she had heard many such cases discussed, with an amazing frankness, during her short stay at the Settlement House. And Jim - Jim with his sleek, patent-leather hair, and his rat-like face - Jim did his work at night! Rose-Marie could not suppress the shudder that ran over her. Quickly she changed the subject to the one bright spot in the Volsky family - to Lily.

"Your little sister," she asked Bennie, "has she always been as she is now? Wasn't there ever a time when she could hear, or speak, or see?"

Bennie winked back a suspicion of tears before he answered. Rose-Marie, who found herself almost forgetting the episode of the kitten, liked him better for the tears. "Yes, Miss," he told her, "she was born all healthy, Ma says. But she had a sickness - when she was a baby. An' she ain't been right since!"

They walked the rest of the way in silence - a silence of untold depth. But it was that silent walk, Rose-Marie felt afterward, that cemented the strange affection that had sprung suddenly into flower between them. As they said good-bye, in front of the brown-stone stoop of the Settlement House, there was none of the usual restraint that exists between a child and a grown-up. And when Rose-Marie asked Bennie, quite as a matter of course, to come to some of their boys' clubs he assented in a manner as casual as her own.

*   *   *   *   *

As she sat down to dinner, that night, Rose-Marie was beaming with happiness and the pride of achievement. The Superintendent, tired after the day's work, noticed her radiance with a wearily sympathetic smile - the Young Doctor, coming in briskly from his round of calls, was aware of her pink cheeks and her sparkling eyes. All at once he realized that Rose-Marie was a distinct addition to the humdrum life of the place; that she was like a sweet old-fashioned garden set down in the gardenless slums. He started to say something of the sort before he remembered that a quarrel lay, starkly, between them.

Rose-Marie, herself, could scarcely have told why she was so bubbling over with gladness. When she left the tenement home of the Volskys she had been exceedingly depressed, when she parted from Bennie at the Settlement House steps she had been ready to cry. But the hours between that parting and dinnertime had brought her a sort of assurance, a sort of joyous bravery. She felt that at last she had found her true vocation, her real place in the sun. The Volsky family presented to her a very genuine challenge.

She glanced, covertly, at the Young Doctor. He was eating soup, and no man is at his best while eating soup. And yet as she watched him, she considered very seriously whether she should tell him of her adventure. His skill might, perhaps, find some way out for Lily, who had not been born a mute, who had come into the world with seeing eyes. Bennie had told her that the child's condition was the result of an illness. Perhaps the Young Doctor might be able to effect at least a partial cure. Perhaps it was selfish of her - utterly, absurdly selfish, to keep the situation to herself.

The Superintendent's voice broke, sharply, into her reverie. It was a pleasant voice, and yet Rose-Marie found herself resenting its questioning tone.

"Did you have a pleasant afternoon, dear?" the Superintendent was asking. "I noticed that you were out for a long while, alone!"

"Why, yes," Rose-Marie faltered, as she spoke, and, to her annoyance, she could feel the red wave of a blush creeping up over her face (Rose-Marie had never learned to control her blushes). "Why, yes, I had a very delightful afternoon!"

The Young Doctor, glancing up from his soup, felt a sudden desire to tease. Rose-Marie, with her cheeks all flushed, made a startlingly colourful, extremely young picture.

"You're blushing!" he told her accusingly. "You're blushing!"

Rose-Marie, feeling the blushes creep still higher, knew a rude impulse to slap the Young Doctor. All of her desire to confide in him died away, as suddenly as it had been born. He was the man who had said that the people who lived in poverty are soulless. He would scoff at the Volskys, and at her desire to help them. Worse than that - he might keep her from seeing the Volskys again. And, in keeping her from seeing them, he would also keep her from making Bennie into a real, wholesome boy - he would keep her from showing Ella the dangers of the precipice that she was skirting. Of course, he might help Lily. But, Rose-Marie told herself that perhaps even Lily - golden-haired, angelic little Lily - might seem soulless to him.

"I'm not blushing, Dr. Blanchard," she said shortly, and could have bitten her tongue for saying it.

The Young Doctor laughed with a boyish vigour.

"I thought," he said annoyingly, "that you were a Christian, Miss Rose-Marie Thompson!"

Rose-Marie felt a tide of quite definite anger rising in her heart.

"I am a Christian!" she retorted.

"Then," the Young Doctor was still laughing, "then you must never, never tell untruths. You are blushing!"

The Superintendent interrupted. It had been her role, lately, to interrupt quarrels between the two who sat on either side of her table.

"Don't tease, Billy Blanchard!" she said, sternly. "If Rose-Marie went anywhere this afternoon, she certainly had a right to. And she also has a right to blush. I'm glad, in these sophisticated days, to see a girl who can blush!"

The Young Doctor was leaning back in his chair, surveying the pair of them with unconcealed amusement.

"How you women do stick together!" he said. "Talk about men being clannish! I believe," he chuckled, "from the way Miss Thompson is blushing, that she's got a very best beau! I believe that she was out with him, this afternoon!"

Rose-Marie, who had always been taught that deceit is wicked, felt a sudden, unexplainable urge to be wicked! She told herself that she hated Dr. Blanchard - she told herself that he was the most unsympathetic of men! His eyes, fixed mirthfully upon her, brought words - that she scarcely meant to say - to her lips.

"Well," she answered slowly and distinctly, "what if I was?"

There was silence for a moment. And then - with something of an effort - the Superintendent spoke.

"I told you," she said, "not to bother Rose-Marie, Doctor. If Rose-Marie was out with a young man I'm sure that she had every right to be. Rose-Marie" - was it possible that her eyes were fixed a shade inquiringly upon the blushing girl - "would have nothing to do with any one who had not been approved by her aunts. And she realizes that she is, in a way, under my care - that I am more or less responsible for her safety and welfare. Rose-Marie is trustworthy, absolutely trustworthy. And she is old enough to take care of herself. You must not bother her, Billy Blanchard!"

It was a long speech for the Superintendent, and it was a kindly one. It was also a speech to invite confidences. But - strangely enough - Rose-Marie could not help feeling that there was a question half concealed in the kindliness of it. She could not help feeling that the Superintendent was just a trifle worried over the prospect of an unknown young man.

It was her time, then, to admit that there was nobody, really - that she had gone out on an adventure by herself, that there had been no "beau." But the consciousness of the Young Doctor's eyes, fixed upon her face, prohibited all speech. She could not tell him about the Volskys - neither could she admit that no young man was interested in her. Every girl wants to seem popular in the eyes of some member of the opposite sex - even though that member may be an unpleasant person - whom she dislikes. And so, with a feeling of utter meanness in her soul - with a real weight of deceit upon her heart - she smiled into the Superintendent's anxious face.

"I do appreciate the way you feel about me," she said softly, "I do, indeed! You may be sure that I won't do anything that either you, or my aunts, would disapprove of!"

After all, she assured herself a trifle uncomfortably, she had in no way told a direct falsehood. They had assumed too much and she had not corrected their assumptions. She said fiercely, in her heart, that she was not to blame if they insisted upon taking things for granted!

IX

AND ANOTHER

As the days crept into weeks, Rose-Marie no longer felt the dull unrest of inaction. She was busy at the Settlement House - her clubs for mothers and young girls, her kindergarten for the little tots, had grown amazingly popular. And at the times when she was not busy at the Settlement House, she had the Volsky family and their many problems to occupy her.

The Volsky family - and their many problems! Rose-Marie would have found it hard to tell which problem was the most important! Of course Lily came first - her infirmities and her sweetness made her the central figure. But the problem of Ella was a more vital one to watch - it was, somehow, more immediate. Rose-Marie had found it hard to reach Ella - except when Lily was the topic of conversation; except when Lily's welfare was to be considered, she stayed silently in the background. But the flashings of her great dark eyes, the quiverings of her too scarlet mouth, were ominous. Rose-Marie could see that the untidiness of the flat, the drunken mutterings of Pa, and her mother's careless-ness and dirt had strained Ella's resistance to the breaking point. Some day there would be a crash and, upon that day Ella would disappear like a gorgeous butterfly that drifts across the road, and out of sight.

Rose-Marie was hoping to push that day into the background - to make it only a dim uncertainty rather than the sword of Damocles that it was. But she could only hope.

Bennie, too, was a problem. But it was Bennie who cheered Rose-Marie when she felt that her efforts in behalf of Ella were failing. For Bennie's brain was the fertile ground in which she could plant ideals, and dreams. Bennie was young enough to change, and easily. He got into the way of waiting for her, after his school had been dismissed, in the little park. And there, seated close together on an iron bench, they would talk; and Rose-Marie would tell endless stories. Most of the stories were about knights who rode upon gallant quests, and about old-time courtesy, and about wonderful animals. But sometimes she told him of her home in the country - of apple trees in bloom, and frail arbutus hiding under the snow. She told him of coasting parties, and bonfires, and trees to climb. And he listened, star-eyed and adoring. They made a pretty picture together - the slim, rosy-cheeked girl and the ragged little boy, with the pale, city sunshine falling, like a mist, all about them.

Lily and Ella and Bennie - Rose-Marie loved them, all three. But Jim Volsky was the unsolvable problem - the one that she tried to push to the back of her mind, to avoid. Mrs. Volsky and Pa she gave up as nearly hopeless - she kept, as much as possible, out of Pa's way, and Mrs. Volsky could only be helped in the attaining of creature comforts - her spirit seemed dead! But Jim insisted upon intruding upon her moments in the flat; he monopolized conversations, and asked impertinent questions, and stared. More than once he had offered to "walk her home" as she was leaving;

Margaret E. Sangster

more than once he had thrust himself menacingly across her path. But she had managed, neatly, to avoid him.

Rose-Marie was afraid of Jim. She admitted it to herself - she even admitted, at times, that the Young Doctor might be of assistance if any emergency should arise out of Jim's sleek persistence. She had noticed, from the first, that the doctor was an impressive man among men - she had seen the encouraging swell of muscles through the warm tweed of his coat sleeve. But to have asked his help in the controlling of Jim would have been an admission of deceit, of weakness, of failure! To prove her own theory that the people were real, underneath - to prove that they had some sort of a code, and worth-while impulses - she had to make the reformation of the Volsky family her own, individual task.

Yes - Rose-Marie was busy. Almost she hated to give up moments of her time to the letters she had to write home - to the sewing that she had to do. She made few friends among the teachers and visitors who thronged the Settlement House by day - she was far too tired, when night came, to meet with the Young Doctor and the Superintendent in the cosy little living-room. But often when her activities lasted well along into the evening, often when her clubs gave sociables or entertainments, she was forced to welcome the Young Doctor (the Superintendent was always welcome); to make room for him beside her own place.

It was during one of these entertainments - her Girls' Sewing Society was giving a party - that she and the Young Doctor had their first real talk. Before the quarrel at the luncheon table they had had little time together; since the quarrel the Young Doctor had seldom been able to corner Rose-Marie. But at the entertainment they were placed, by the hand of circumstance, upon a wooden settee in the back of the room. And there, for the better part of two hours - while Katie Syrop declaimed poetry and Helen Merskovsky played upon the piano, and others recited long and monotonous dialogues - they were forced to stay.

The Young Doctor was in a chastened mood. He applauded heartily whenever a part of the program came to a close; the comments that he made behind his hand were neither sarcastic nor condescending. He praised the work that Rose-Marie had done and then, while she was glowing - almost against her will - from the warmth of that praise, he ventured a remark that had nothing to do with the work.

"When I see you," he told her very seriously, "when I see you, sitting here in one of our gray coloured meeting rooms, I can't help thinking how appropriate your name is. Rose-Marie - there's a flower, isn't there, that's named Rosemary? I like flowery names!"

Rose-Marie laughed, as lightly as she could, to cover a strange feeling of embarrassment.

"Most people don't like them," she said - "flowery names, I mean. I don't myself. I like names like Jane, and Anne, and Nancy. I like names like Phyllis and Sarah. I've always felt that my first name didn't fit my last one. Thompson," she was warming to her subject, "is such a matter-of-fact name. There's no romance in it. But Rose-Marie -"

Margaret E. Sangster

The Young Doctor interrupted.

"But Rose-Marie," he finished for her, "is teeming with romance! It suggests vague perfumes, and twilight in the country, and gay little lights shining through the dusk. It suggests poetry."

Rose-Marie had folded her hands, softly, in her lap. Her eyes were bent upon them.

"My mother," she said, and her voice was quiet and tender, "loved poetry. I've heard how she used to read it every afternoon, in her garden. She loved perfumes, too, and twilight in the country. My mother was the sort of a woman who would have found the city a bit hard, I think, to live in. Beauty meant such a lot - to her. She gave me my name because she thought, just as you think, that it had a hint of lovely things in it. And, even though I sometimes feel that I'd like a plainer one, I can't be sorry that she gave it to me. For it was a part of her - a gift that was built out of her imagination," all at once she coughed, perhaps to cover the slight tremor in her voice, and then -

"To change the subject," she said, "I'll tell you what Rosemary really is. You said that you thought it was a flower. It's more than a flower," she laughed shakily, "it's a sturdy, evergreeny sort of little shrub. It has a clean fragrance, a trifle like mint. And it bears small blue blossoms. Folk say that it stands for remembrance," suddenly her eyes were down, again, upon her clasped hands. "Let's stop talking about flowers and the country - and mothers - " she said suddenly. Her voice broke upon the last word.

The Young Doctor's understanding glance was on the

girl's down-bent face. After a moment he spoke.

"Are you ever sorry that you left the home town, Miss Rose-Marie?" he questioned.

Rose-Marie looked at him, for a moment, to see whether he was serious. And then, as no flicker of mirth stirred his mouth, she answered.

"Sometimes I'm homesick," she said. "Usually after the lights are out, at night. But I'm never sorry!"

The Young Doctor was staring off into space - past the raised platform where the girls of the club were performing.

"I wonder," he said, after a moment, "I wonder if you can imagine what it is to have nothing in the world to be lonesome for, Miss Rose-Marie?"

Rose-Marie felt a quick wave of sympathy toward him.

"My mother and my father are dead, Dr. Blanchard - you know that," she told him, "but my aunts have always been splendid," she added honestly, "and I have any number of friends! No, I've never felt at all alone!"

The Young Doctor was silent for a moment. And then -

"It isn't an alone feeling that I mean," he told her, "not exactly! It's rather an empty feeling! Like hunger, almost. You see my father and mother are dead, too. I can't even remember them. And I never had any aunts to be splendid to me. My childhood - even my babyhood - was spent in an orphan asylum with a firm-fisted matron who punished me; with nobody to give me the love I needed. I came out of it a hard man - at fourteen. I - " he broke off, suddenly, and then -

"I don't know why I'm telling you all this," he said; "you wouldn't be in the least interested in my school days - they were pretty drab! And you wouldn't be interested in the scholarship that gave me my profession. For," his tone changed slightly, "you aren't even interested in the result - not enough to try to understand my point of view, when I attempt to tell you, frankly, just what I think of the people down here - barring girls like these," he pointed to the stage, "and a few others who are working hard to make good! You act, when I say that they're like animals, as if I'm giving you a personal insult! You think, when I suggest that you don't go, promiscuously, into dirty tenements, that I'm trying to curb your ambition - to spoil your chances of doing good! But I'm not, really. I'm only endeavouring, for your own protection, to give you the benefit of my rather bitter experience. I don't want any one so young, and trusting and - yes, beautiful - as you are, to be forced by experience into my point of view. We love having you here, at the Settlement House. But I almost wish that you'd go home - back to the place and the people that you're lonesome for - after the lights are out!"

Rose-Marie, watching the play of expression across his keen dark face, was struck, first of all by his sincerity. It was only after a moment that she began to feel the old resentment creeping back.

"Then," she said at last, very slowly, "then you think that I'm worthless here? It seems to me that I can help the people more, just because I am fresh, and untried, and not in the least bitter! It seems to me that by direct contact with them I may be able to show them the tender, guiding hand of God - as it has always been revealed to me. But you think that I'm worthless!"

There was a burst of loud singing from the raised platform. The girls of the sewing club loved to sing. But neither Rose-Marie nor the Young Doctor was conscious of it.

"No," the Young Doctor answered, also very slowly, "no, I don't think that you are worthless - not at all.-But I'm almost inclined to think that you're *wasted*. Go home, child, go home to the little town! Go home before the beautiful colour has worn off the edge of your dreams!"

Again Rose-Marie felt the swift burst of anger that she had felt upon other occasions. Why did he persist in treating her like a child? But her voice was steady as she answered.

"Well," she said, "I'm afraid that I'll have to disappoint you! For I came here with a definite plan to carry out. And I'm going to stay here until I've at least partly made good!"

The Young Doctor was watching her flushed face. He answered almost regretfully.

"Then," he said, "I'm glad that you have a sweetheart - you didn't deny it, you know, the other night! He'll take you away from the slums, I reckon, before very long! He'll take you away before you've been hurt!"

Rose-Marie, looking straight ahead, did not answer. But the weight of deceit upon her soul made her feel

Margaret E. Sangster

very wicked.

Yes, the weight of deceit upon her soul made her feel very wicked! But later that night, after the club members had gone home, dizzy with many honours, it was not the weight of deceit that troubled her. As she crept into her narrow little bed she was all at once very sorry for herself; and for a vanished dream! Dr. Blanchard could be so nice - when he wanted to. He could be so understanding, so sympathetic! There on the bench in the rear of the room they had been, for a moment, very close together. She had nearly come back, during their few minutes of really intimate conversation, to her first glowing impression of him. And then he had changed so suddenly - had so abruptly thrust aside the little house of friendship that they had begun to build. "If he would only let me," she told herself, "I could teach him to like the things I like. If he would only understand I could explain just how I feel about people. If he would only give me a chance I could keep him from being so lonely."

Rose-Marie had known few men. The boys of her own town she scarcely regarded as men - they were old playmates, that was all. No one stood out from the other, they were strikingly similar. They had carried her books to school, had shared apples with her, had played escort to prayer-meetings and to parties. But none of them had ever stirred her imagination as the Young Doctor stirred it.

There in the dark Rose-Marie felt herself blushing. Could it be possible that she felt an interest in the Young Doctor, an interest that was more than a casual interest? Could it be possible that she liked a man who showed plainly, upon every possible occasion, that he did not like her? Could it be possible that a person who read sensational stories, who did not believe in the greatness of human nature, who refused to go to church, attracted her?

Of a sudden she had flounced out of bed; had shrugged her slender little body into a shapeless wrapper - the parting gift of a girl friend - from which her small flushed face seemed to grow like some delicate spring blossom. With hurried steps - she might almost have been running away from something - she crossed the room to a small table that served as a combination dresser and writing desk. Brushing aside her modest toilet articles, she reached for a pad of paper and a small business-like fountain pen. Her aunts - she wanted them, all at once, and badly. She wished that she might talk with them - writing seemed so inadequate.

"My dears," she began, "I miss you very much. Often I'm lonely enough to cry. Of course," she added hastily (for they must not worry), "of course, every one is nice to me. I like every one, too. That is, except Dr. Blanchard. I guess I told you about him; he's the resident physician. He's awfully good looking but he's not very pleasant. I never hated any one so -" she paused, for a moment, as a round tear splashed devastatingly down upon the paper.

X

MRS. VOLSKY PROMISES TO TRY

As Lily pattered across the room, on her soft, almost noiseless little feet, Rose-Marie stopped talking. She had been having one of her rare conversations alone with Mrs. Volsky - a conversation that she had almost schemed for - and yet she stopped. It struck her suddenly as strange that Lily's presence in any place should make such a vast difference - that the child should bring with her a healing silence and a curious tenderness. She had felt, many times before, a slowing up in conversations - she had seen the bitterness drain from Ella's face, the stolidness from Bennie's. She had even seen Pa, half intoxicated, turn and go quietly from a room that Lily was entering. And now, as she watched, she saw a spark leap into the dullness of Mrs. Volsky's eyes.

With a gentle hand she reached out to the child, drew her close. Lily nestled against her side with a slight smile upon her faintly coral lips, with her blue, vacant gaze fixed upon space - or upon something that they could not see! Rose-Marie had often felt that Lily was watching beautiful vistas with those sightless eyes of hers; that she was hearing wonderful sounds, with her useless little ears - sounds that normal people could not hear. But she did not say anything of the sort to Mrs.

Volsky - Mrs. Volsky would not have been able to understand. Instead she spoke of something else that had lain, for a long time, upon her mind.

"Has Lily ever received any medical attention?" she asked abruptly.

Mrs. Volsky's face took on lines of blankness. "What say?" she mouthed thickly. "I don' understan'?"

Rose-Marie reconstructed her question.

"Has Lily ever been taken to a doctor?" she asked.

Mrs. Volsky answered more quickly than she usually answered questions.

"When she was first sick, years ago," she told Rose-Marie, "she had a doctor then. He say - no help fer her. Las' year Ella, she took Lily by a free clinic. But the doctors, there, they say Lily never get no better. And if there comes another doctor to our door, now -" she shrugged; and her shrug seemed to indicate the uselessness of all doctors.

Rose-Marie, with suddenly misting eyes, lifted Lily to her knee... "The only times," she said slowly, "when I feel any doubt in my mind of the Divine Plan - are the times when I see little children, who have never done anything at all wicked or wrong, bearing pain and suffering and..." she broke off.

Mrs. Volsky answered, as she almost always answered, with a mechanical question.

"What say?" she murmured dully.

Rose-Marie eyed her over the top of Lily's golden head. After all, she told herself, in the case of Mrs. Volsky she could see the point of Dr. Blanchard's assertion! She had known many animals who apparently were quicker to reason, who apparently had more enthusiasm and ambition, than Mrs. Volsky. She looked at the dingy apron, the unkempt hair, the sagging flesh upon the gray cheeks. And she was conscious suddenly of a feeling of revulsion. She fought it back savagely.

"Christ," she told herself, "never turned away from people because they were dirty, or ugly, or stupid. Christ loved everybody - no matter how low they were. He would have loved Mrs. Volsky."

It was curious how it gave her strength - that reflection - strength to look straight at the woman in front of her, and to smile.

"Why," she asked, and the smile became brighter as she asked it, "why don't you try to fix your hair more neatly, Mrs. Volsky? And why don't you wear fresh aprons, and keep the flat cleaner? Why don't you try to make your children's home more pleasant for them?"

Mrs. Volsky did not resent the suggestion as some other women might have done. Mrs. Volsky had reached the point where she no longer resented even blows.

"I uster try - onct," she said tonelessly, "but it ain't no good, no more. Ella an' Bennie an' Jim don' care. An' Pa - he musses up th' flat whenever he comes inter it. An' Lily can't see how it looks. So what's th' use?"

It was a surprisingly long speech for Mrs. Volsky. And some of it showed a certain reasoning power. Rose-Marie told herself, in all fairness, that if she were Mrs. Volsky - she, too, might be inclined to ask "What's th' use?" She leaned forward, searching desperately in her mind for something to say.

"Do you like *me*, Mrs. Volsky?" she questioned at last, "Do you like me?"

The woman nodded, and again the suggestion of a light flamed up in her eyes.

"Sure I like you," she said, "you are good to all of us - *an' to Lily*."

"Then," Rose-Marie's voice was quivering with eagerness, "then won't you try - *for my sake* - to make things here," the sweep of her hand included every corner of the ugly room, "a little better? I'll help you, very gladly. I'll make new aprons for you, and I'll" - her brave resolution faltered, but only for a moment - "I'll wash your hair, and take you to the free baths with me. And then," she had a sudden inspiration, "then Lily will love to touch you, you'll be so nice and clean! Then Lily will be glad that she has you for a mother!"

All at once the shell of stupidity had slipped from Mrs. Volsky's bent shoulders. All at once she was eager, breathlessly eager.

"Miss," she said, and one thin, dingy hand was laid appealingly upon Rose-Marie's dress, "Miss, you can do wit' me as you wish to! If you t'ink dat my bein' clean will make Lily glad" - she made a sudden impetuous gesture with her hand - "den I will be clean!

If you t'ink dat she will like better dat I should be her mother," the word, on her lips, was surprisingly sweet, "den I will do - *anyt'ing*!" All at once she broke into phrases that were foreign to Rose-Marie, phrases spoken lovingly in some almost forgotten tongue. And the girl knew that she was quite forgotten - that the drab woman was dreaming over some youthful hope, was voicing tenderly the promises of a long dead yesterday, and was making an impassioned pledge to her small daughter and to the future! The words that she spoke might be in the language of another land - but the tone was unmistakable, was universal.

Rose-Marie, listening to her, felt a sudden desire to kneel there, on the dirty tenement floor, and say a little prayer of thanksgiving. Once again she had proved that she was right - and that the Young Doctor was wrong.

XI

BENNIE COMES TO THE SETTLEMENT HOUSE

It was Bennie who came first to the Settlement House. Shyly, almost, he slipped through the great doors - as one who seeks something that he does not quite understand. As he came, a gray kitten, creeping out from the shadows of the hall, rubbed affectionately against his leg. And Bennie, half unconsciously - and with absolutely no recognition - stooped to pat its head. Rose-Marie would have cried with joy to have seen him do it, but Rose-Marie was in another part of the building, teaching tiny children to embroider outlines, with gay wool, upon perforated bits of cardboard. The Young Doctor, passing by the half-opened door of the kindergarten room, saw her there and paused for a moment to enjoy the sight. He thought, with a curious tightening of his lips, as he left noiselessly, that some day Rose-Marie would be surrounded by her own children - far away from the Settlement House. And he was surprised at the sick feeling that the thought gave him.

"I've been rather a fool," he told himself savagely, "trying to send her away. I've been a fool. But I'd never known anything like her - not in all of my life! And it makes me shiver to think of what one meeting with some unscrupulous gangster would do to her point of view. It makes me want to fight the world when I realize how an unpleasant experience would affect her love of people. I'd rather never see her again," he was surprised, for a second time, at the pain that the words caused him, "than to have her made unhappy. I hope that this man of hers is a regular fellow!"

He passed on down the hall. He walked slowly, the vision of Rose-Marie, a dream child held close to her breast, before his eyes. That was why, perhaps, he did not see Bennie - why he stumbled against the boy.

"Hello," he said gruffly, for his voice was just a trifle hoarse (voices get that way sometimes, when visions *will* stay in front of one's eyes!) "Hello, youngster! Do you want anything? Or are you just looking around?"

Bennie straightened up. The kitten that he had been patting rubbed reassuringly against his legs, but Bennie needed more reassurance than the affection of a kitten can give. The kindness of Rose-Marie, the stories that she had told him, had given him a great deal of confidence. But he had not yet learned to stand up, fearlessly, to a big man with a gruff voice. It is a step forward to have stopped hurting the smaller things. But to accept a pretty lady's assurance that things larger than you will be kind - that is almost too much to expect! Bennie answered just a shade shrinkingly.

"Th' kids in school," he muttered, "tol' me 'bout a club they come to here. It's a sort of a Scout Club. They wears soldier clo's. An' they does things fer people. An' I wanter b'long," he gulped, noisily.

The Young Doctor leaned against the wall. He did not realize how tall and strong he looked, leaning there, or he could not have smiled so whimsically. To him the small dark boy with his earnest face, standing beside the gray kitten, was just an interesting, rather lovable joke.

"Which do you want most," he questioned, "to wear soldier clothes, or to do things for people?"

Bennie gulped again, and shuffled his feet. His voice came, at last, rather thickly.

"I sorter want to do things fer people!" he said.

More than anything else the Young Doctor hated folk, even children, who say or do things for effect. And he knew well the lure that soldier clothes hold for the small boy.

"Say, youngster," he inquired in a not too gentle voice, "are you trying to bluff me? Or do you really mean what you're saying? And if you do - why?"

Bennie had never been a quitter. By an effort he steadied his voice.

"I mean," he said, "what I'm a-tellin' yer. I wanter be a good boy. My pa, he drinks. He drinks like - " The word he used, in description, was not the sort of a word that should have issued from childish lips. "An' my big brother - he ain't like Pa, but he's a bum, too! I don't wanter be like they are - not if I kin help it! I wanter be th' sort of a guy King Arthur was, an' them knights of his'n. I wanter be like that there St. George feller, as killed dragons. I wanter do real things," unconsciously he was quoting from the gospel of Rose-Marie, "wi' my life! I wanter be a good husban' an' father - "

Margaret E. Sangster

All at once the Young Doctor was laughing. It was not an unkind laugh - it gave Bennie heart to listen to it - but it was exceedingly mirthful. Bennie could not know that the idea of himself, as a husband and father, was sending this tall man into such spasms of merriment - he could not know that it was rather incongruous to picture his small grubby form in the shining armour of St. George or of King Arthur. But, being glad that the doctor was not angry, he smiled too - his strange, twisted little smile.

The Young Doctor stopped laughing almost as quickly as he had begun. With something of interest in his face he surveyed the little ragged boy.

"Where," he questioned after a moment, "did you learn all of that stuff about knights, and saints, and doing things with your life, and husbands and fathers? Who told you about it?"

Bennie hesitated a moment. Perhaps he was wondering who had given this stranger a right to pry into his inner shrine. Perhaps he was wondering if Rose-Marie would like an outsider to know just what she had told him. When he answered, his answer was evasive.

"A lady told me," he said. "A lady."

The Young Doctor was laughing again.

"And I suppose," he remarked, with an effort at solemnity, "that gentlemen don't pass ladies' names about between 'em - I suppose that you wouldn't tell me who this lady of yours may be, even though I'd like to meet her?"

Bennie's lips closed in a hard little line that quirked up at one end. He shook his head.

"I'd ruther not," he said very slowly. "Say - Where's th' Scout Club?"

The Young Doctor shook his head.

"It's such a strange, old-fashioned, young person!" he informed the empty hallway. And then - "Come with me, youngster," he said kindly, "and we'll find this very wonderful club where small boys learn about doing things for people - and, incidentally, wear soldier clothes!"

Bennie, following stealthily behind him, felt that he had found another friend - something like his lady, only different!

Margaret E. Sangster

XII

AN ISLAND

Rose-Marie was exceptionally weary that night. It had been a hard day. All three of her classes had met, and - late in the afternoon - she had made good her promise to wash Mrs. Volsky's hair. The task had not been a joyous one - she felt that she could never wash hair again - not even her own soft curls or the fine, snowy locks that crowned her aunts' stately heads. Mrs. Volsky had once more relapsed into her shell of silence - she had seemed more apathetic, more dull than ever. But Rose-Marie had noticed that there were no unwashed dishes lying in the tub - that the corners of the room had had some of the grime of months swept out of them. When Ella Volsky came suddenly into the flat, with lips compressed, and a high colour, Rose-Marie had been glowingly conscious of her start of surprise. And when she had said, haltingly, in reference to the hair - "I'll dry it for you, Miss Rose-Marie!" Rose-Marie could have wept with happiness. It was the first time that she had ever heard Ella offer to do anything for her mother.

Jim - coming in as she was about to leave - had added to Rose-Marie's weariness. He had been more insistent than usual - he had commented upon her rosy cheeks and he had made a laughing reference to her wide eyes.

And he had asked her, gruffly, why she didn't take up with some feller like himself - a good provider, an' all, that'd doll her up the way she'd oughter be dolled up? And when Ella had interrupted, her dark eyes flashing, he had told her - with a burst of soul-chilling profanity - to mind her own business.

And then Pa had come in - apparently more drunk than he had ever been. And Rose-Marie had seen his bleary eyes pass, without a flicker of interest, over his wife's clean apron and freshly washed hair; had seen him throw his coat and his empty bottle into one of the newly dusted corners, had seen his collapse into a heap in the center of the room. And, last of all, as she had hurried away, with Jim's final insinuation ringing in her ears, she had known the fear that all was not well with Bennie - for Bennie came in every afternoon before she left. She could not know that Bennie, by this time a budding Boy Scout, was learning more lessons of the sort that she had taught him.

Yes, she was weary, in every fibre of her being, as she sat down to supper that night. She had it quite alone in the dining-room, which, all at once, seemed very large - for the Superintendent was sitting, somewhere, with a dying woman, and the Young Doctor had been called out on an emergency case. And then, still alone, she wandered into the library of the Settlement House and picked up a book. She felt, somehow, too tired to sleep - too utterly exhausted to lay her head upon her pillow. It was in the library that the Superintendent, coming wearily back from the watch with death, found her.

"My dear," said the Superintendent, and there was a sound of tears in her usually steady voice, "my dear, I'm about all in! Yes, I know it's slang, but I can't help it - I feel slangy! Come up to my sitting-room for a few minutes and we'll have a cup of hot chocolate!"

Rose-Marie laid down her book with alacrity. She realized, suddenly, that she wanted companionship of her own sort - that she longed with all of her soul to chat with some one who did not murder the queen's English, that she wanted to exchange commonplaces about books, and music, and beautiful things - things that the Volskys would not understand.

"I guess," she said, as she followed the Superintendent into the cozy sitting-room, "I guess that tiredness is in the air to-day. I'm all in, myself. A cup of chocolate and a friendly talk will be a godsend to me, this evening!"

The Superintendent was laying aside her coat and her hat. She smoothed her hair with a nervous hand, and straightened her linen collar, before she sank into an easy chair.

"Child," she said abruptly, "*you* shouldn't be tired - not ever! You've got youth, and all of the world at your feet. You've got beauty, and confidence, and faith. And I - well, I'm getting to be an old woman! I feel some-times as if I've been sitting on the window sill, watching life go by, for centuries. You mustn't - " She paused, and there was a sudden change in her voice, "You're not tiring yourself, Rose-Marie? You're not doing more than your strength will permit? If you could have read the letter that your aunts sent to me, when you first came to the Settlement House! I tell you, child, I've felt my responsibility keenly! I'd no more think of letting you brush up against the sort of facts I'm facing, than I would -"

Rose-Marie's cheeks were flushed, her eyes were bright, as she interrupted.

"Somehow," she said, "I can't think that you and my aunts are quite right about shielding me - about keeping me from brushing up against life, and the real facts of life. It seems to me that there's only one way to develop - really. And that way is to learn to accept things as they come; to meet situations - no matter how appalling they may be, with one's eyes open. If I," she was warming to her subject, "am never to tire myself out, working for others, how am I to help them? If I am never to see conditions as they are how am I ever to know the sort of a problem that we, here at the Settlement House, are fighting? Dr. Blanchard wouldn't try to treat a case if he had no knowledge of medicine - he wouldn't try to set a broken leg if he had never studied anatomy. You wouldn't be in charge, here, if you didn't know the district, if you didn't realize the psychological reasons back of the things that the people of the district say and do. Without the knowledge that you're trying to keep from me you'd be as useless as" - she faltered - "as I am!"

The Superintendent's expression reflected all the tenderness of her nature; the mother-instinct, which she had never known, made her smile into the girl's serious face.

"My dear," she said, "you must not think that you're useless. You must never think that! Look at the success you've had in your club work - remember how the children that you teach have come to love you. You've done more with them, because of the things that you don't know, than I could ever do - despite the hard facts that I've had to brush up against. Find content, dear, in being the sweet place in our garden - that has so pitifully few flowers. Do not long for the hard, uncomfortable places on the other side of the garden wall!"

Despite the Superintendent's expression - despite the gentle tone of her voice, Rose-Marie felt a sudden desire to cry out against the irony of it all. She was so tired of being classed with the flowers! "They toil not, neither do they spin," came back to her, from a certain golden text that she had learned, long ago, in Sunday-school. Even at the time it had seemed to her as if the flowers enjoyed lives that were a shade too easy! At the time it had seemed unfair that they, who were not workers, should be beautiful - more beautiful than the ants, for instance, that uncomplainingly toiled all day long for their existence.

"I don't want to be a flower," she exclaimed, almost fretfully, "I want to be a worth while member of society - that's what I want! What's the use of being a decoration in a garden! What's the use of knowing only the sunshine? I want to know storms, too, and gales of wind. I want to share the tempests that you go through!" She hesitated; and then - "I read a book once," she said slowly, "I forget what it was - but I remember, in one place, that a woman was being discussed. She was a very beautiful elderly woman who, despite her age, had a face as unlined and calm as a young girl's face could be. One character in the book commented upon the woman's youth and charm, and another character agreed that she *was* beautiful and charming, but that she'd be worth more if she had a few lines on her face. 'She's never known tears,' the character said, 'she's never lived *deeply* enough to know tears! Her life has been just a surface life. If you go down deep enough into the earth you find water, always. If you go down deep enough into life you invariably find tears. It's one of the unbreakable rules!'" Rose-Marie paused, for a moment, and stole a covert glance at the Superintendent's face. "You don't want me to be a woman whose life is only a surface life," she pleaded, "and it will be just that if you keep me from helping, as I want to help! You don't want me to have a perfectly unlined face when I'm eighty years old?"

All at once the Superintendent was laughing. "You child!" she exclaimed when the first spasm of mirth had passed, "you blessed child! If you could know how ridiculously young you looked, sitting there and talking about lined faces - and yourself at eighty. Eighty is a long way off, Rose-Marie - for you!"

The girl joined, a trifle shamefacedly, in the older woman's laughter.

"I reckon," she agreed, "that I do take myself too seriously! But - well, there are families that I'm just dying to help - families that I've come in contact with through the" - again she was forced to a slight deceit - "through the Settlement House. I'm sure that I could help them if you'd let me visit them, in their own homes. I'm sure that I'd be able to reform ever so many people if you'd only let me go out and find them. The city missionary who spoke once in our church, back home, told of wonderful things that he'd done - of lives that he'd actually made over. Of course, I couldn't do the sort of work he did, but I'm sure - if you'd only give me a chance -" She paused.

The Superintendent was silent for a moment.

And then -

"Maybe you're right, dear," she said, "and maybe you're wrong. Maybe I am cramping your ambitions - maybe I am hampering your mental and spiritual growth. But then, again, maybe I'm right! And I'm inclined to think that I am right. I'm inclined to adhere to my point, that it will be better for you to wait, until you're older, before you go into many tenements - before you do much reforming outside of the Settlement House. When you're older and more experienced I'll be glad to let you do anything -"

She was interrupted by a rap upon the door. It was a gentle rap, but it was, above all, a masculine one. There was real gladness on her face as she rose to answer it.

"I didn't expect Billy Blanchard - he thought he had an all-night case," she told Rose-Marie. "How nice!"

But Rose-Marie was rising to her feet.

"I don't think that I'll stay," she said hurriedly, "I'm too tired, after all! I think -"

The Superintendent had paused in her progress to the door. Her voice was surprisingly firm, of a sudden; firmer than Rose-Marie had ever heard it.

"No, my dear," said the Superintendent, "you're not too tired! You just don't want to be civil to a very fine boy - who has had a harder day than either of us. You came to the slums, Rose-Marie, to help people - to show that you were a Christian. I think that you can show it, to-night, by forgetting a silly quarrel that happened weeks ago - by forgetting the words Dr. Blanchard said that he never really meant, inside. If he thought that these people weren't worth it, do you suppose he'd stay here, at the Settlement House, for a mere pittance? He's had many a chance to go to fashionable hospitals, up-town!"

Rose-Marie, bewildered, and not a little ashamed, sank back into her seat as the Superintendent swung open the door.

The Young Doctor came in with a springing step, but there were gray lines that spoke of extreme fatigue about his mouth, and his eyes were darkly circled. His surprise, at the sight of Rose-Marie, was evident - though he tried to hide it by the breeziness of his manner.

"You'll be glad to know," he told the Superintendent, "that the stork has called on the Stefan family. It's a boy - nine pounds - with lots of dark hair. There have been three girls, in the Stefan family," he explained to Rose-Marie, "and so they are wild with joy at this latest addition. Papa Stefan is strutting about like a proud turkey, with his chest out. And Mamma Stefan is trying to sing a lullaby. I feel something like a tool in the hand of Providence, to-night!" He threw himself upon the sofa.

There was deep, motherly affection in the Superintendent's face as she smiled at him.

"We're all of us mental and physical wrecks this evening, Billy!" she said. "I think that I've never been so utterly worn out before. Katie" (Katie was the stolid maid) "is making chocolate for us!"

"Chocolate!" The Young Doctor's glance answered the affection that shone out of the Superintendent's face - "You *are* a dear!" He smiled at her, and then - all at once - turned swiftly to Rose-Marie.

"Don't let's squabble to-night," he said childishly, "not about anything! We're dog-tired, all three of us, and we're not up to even a tiny quarrel. I'm willing to admit anything you want me to - even that I'm wrong on a lot of subjects. And I want you to admit, yourself, that you'd rather be here, with the two of us, than out in some den of iniquity - reforming people. Am I right?"

Rose-Marie felt a glow of friendship toward the Young Doctor. Why couldn't he always be like this - confiding and boyish and approachable? She smiled at him, very sweetly, as she answered.

"You're right," she admitted. "I'm afraid that I haven't the heart to think of reforming any one, this evening! I'm just glad - glad from the very soul of me - to be here with you all, in the very center of this - island!"

The Superintendent's face was puzzled - the Superintendent's eyes were vague - as she asked a question.

"You said - *island*?" she questioned.

Rose-Marie laughed with a shade of embarrassment.

"I didn't really mean to say island," she explained, "but - well, you remember what Dr. Blanchard told us, once, about the little bugs that fastened together - first one and then another until there were billions? And how, at last, they made an island?" She paused and, at their nods of assent, went on. "Ever since then," she told them slowly, "I've thought of us, here at the Settlement House, as the first little bugs - the ones that the others must hold to. And I've felt, though many of them don't realize it, though we hardly realize it ourselves, that we're building an island together - *an island of faith*!"

There was silence for a moment. And then the Young Doctor spoke. His voice was a trifle husky.

"You've made me more than a bit ashamed of myself, Miss Rose-Marie," he said, "and I want to thank you for putting a real symbolism into my chance words. After all" - suddenly he laughed, and then - "after all," he said, "I wouldn't be surprised if you are right! I had a curious experience, this afternoon, that would go to prove your theory."

The Superintendent was leaning back, shielding her eyes from the light. "Tell us about your experience, Billy," she said.

The chocolate had come, and the Young Doctor took an appreciative sip before he answered.

"Just as I was going out this afternoon," he said, at last, "I ran into a dirty little boy in the hall. He was fondling a kitten - that thin gray one that you brought to the Settlement House, Miss Rose-Marie. I asked him what he was doing and he told me that he was hunting for a Scout Club that he'd heard about. I" - the Young Doctor chuckled - "I engaged him in conversation. And he told me that his ambition was to be a combination of St. George and King Arthur and all the rest of those fellows. He said that, some day, he wanted to be a good husband and father. When I asked him where he got his large ambitions he told me that a lady had given them to him."

Rose-Marie was leaning forward. "Did he tell you the lady's name?" she breathed.

The Young Doctor shook his head.

"Not a thing did he tell me!" he said dramatically. "The lady's name seemed to be something in the nature of a sacred trust to him. But his big dark eyes were full of the spirit that she'd given him. And his funny little crooked mouth was - " He paused, suddenly, his gaze fixed upon Rose-Marie. "What's the matter?" he queried. "What's the matter? You look as if some-body'd just left you a million dollars!"

Rose-Marie's face was flushed and radiant. Her eyes were deep wells of joy.

"I have every reason in the world," she said softly, "to be happy!" And she was too absorbed in her own thoughts to realize that a sudden cloud had crept across the brightness of the Young Doctor's face.

XIII

ELLA MAKES A DECISION

And then the climax of Ella's life - the crash that Rose-Marie had been expecting - happened. It happened when Ella came furiously into the Volsky flat, early one afternoon, and - ignoring the little Lily, who sat placidly on Rose-Marie's lap - hurried silently into her own room. Mrs. Volsky, bending over the wash-tubs, straightened up as if she could almost feel the electric quality of the air, as Ella passed her, but Rose-Marie only held tighter to Lily - as if, somehow, the slim little body gave her comfort.

"I wonder what's the matter?" she ventured, after a moment.

Mrs. Volsky, again bending over the wash-tubs, answered.

"Ella, she act so funny, lately," she told Rose-Marie, "an' there is some feller; Bennie, he tell me that he have seen her wit' some feller! A rich feller, maybe; maybe he puts Ella up to her funny business!"

There were sounds of activity from the inner room, as if clothing was being torn down from hooks - as if heavy garments were being flung into bags.

Margaret E. Sangster

Rose-Marie listened, apprehensively, to the sounds before she spoke again.

"Perhaps I'd better go in and see what's the matter," she suggested.

Mrs. Volsky, looking back over her shoulder, gave a helpless little shrug. "If you t'inks best," she said hopelessly. "But Ella - she not never want to take any help..."

Only too well Rose-Marie knew what Mrs. Volsky meant by her twisted sentence. Only too well she understood that Ella would never allow herself to be biased by another's judgment, - that Ella would not allow herself to be moved by another's plea. And yet she set Lily gently down upon the floor and rose to her feet.

"I'll see what she's doing," she told Mrs. Volsky, and pushed open the inner door.

Despite all of the time that she had spent in the Volsky flat, Rose-Marie had never been past the front room with its tumbled heaps of bedding, and its dirt. She was surprised to see that the inner room, shared by Ella and Lily, was exquisitely neat, though tiny. There were no windows - the only light came from a rusty gas fixture - but Rose-Marie, after months in the slums, was prepared for that. It was the geranium, blooming on the shabby table, that caught her eye; it was the clean hair-brush, lying on the same table, and the framed picture of a Madonna, upon the wall, that attracted her. She spoke of them, first, to the girl who knelt on the floor, packing a cheap suit-case - spoke of them before she questioned gently:

"You're not going away, are you, Ella?"

Ella glanced up from her packing.

"Yes. I'm going away!" she said, shortly. And then, as if against her will, she added:

"I got th' flower an' th' picture for Lily. Oh, sure, I know that she can't see 'em! But I sorter feel that she knows they're here!"

Rose-Marie's voice was very soft, as she spoke again.

"I'm glad that you chose the picture you did," she said, "the picture of the Christ Child and His Mother!"

Ella wadded a heavy dress into the suit-case.

"I don't hold much with religious pictures," she said, without looking up; "religion never did much fer me! I only got it 'cause th' Baby had hair like Lily's hair!"

Rose-Marie crouched down, suddenly, upon the floor beside the girl. She laid her hand upon the suit-case.

"Where are you going, Ella?" she asked abruptly. "Where are you going - and when will you be back?"

Ella's lips drew up into the semblance of a smile - a very bitter one - as she answered.

"It's none of yer business where I'm goin'," she said, "an' I may not ever come back - see?"

Rose-Marie caught her breath in a kind of sob. It was as she had guessed - and feared!

"Ella," she asked slowly, "are you going alone?"

The girl's face coloured swiftly, with a glorious wave of crimson. She tossed her head with a defiant movement.

"No, I ain't goin' alone!" she told Rose-Marie. "You kin betcha life I ain't goin' alone!"

Rose-Marie - sitting beside her on the floor - asked God, silently, for help before she spoke again. She felt suddenly powerless, futile.

"*Why* are you going, dear?" she questioned, at last.

Ella dropped the shoes that she had been about to tuck into the suit-case. Her eyes were grim.

"Because," she said, "I'm tired of all o' this," Her finger pointed in the direction of the outer room. "I'm tired o' dirt, and drunken people, and Jim's rotten talk. I'm tired o' meals et out o' greasy dishes, an' cheap clothes, and jobs that I hate - an' that I can't nohow seem ter hold! I'm tired, dog-tired, o' life. All that's ever held me in this place is Lily. An' sometimes, when I look at her, I don't think that she'd know the difference whether I was here 'r not!"

Rose-Marie was half sobbing in her earnestness.

"Ah, but she would know the difference," she cried. "Lily loves you with all of her heart. And your mother is really trying to be neater, to make a better home for you! She hasn't a pleasant time of it, either - your mother. But she doesn't run away. She stays!"

There was scorn in the laugh that came, all at once, from Ella's twisted mouth. Her great eyes were somberly sarcastic.

"Sure, she stays," said Ella, "'cause she ain't got enough gumption ter be gettin' out! I know."

In her heart Rose-Marie was inclined to agree with Ella. She knew, herself, that Mrs. Volsky would never have the courage to make any sort of a definite decision. But she couldn't say so - not while Ella was staring at her with that cynical expression.

"I guess," she said bravely, "that we'd better leave your mother out of this discussion. After all, it's between you - and your conscience."

"Say," Ella's face was suddenly drawn and ugly, "say, where do you get off to pull this conscience stuff? You've always had a nice home, an' pretty clothes, an' clean vittles, an' - an' love! I ain't had any of it. But," her eyes flamed, "I'm goin' to! Don't you dast ter pull this conscience stuff on me - I've heard you profess'nal slummers talk before - a lot o' times. What good has a conscience ever done me - huh?"

Rose-Marie had been watching the girl's face. Of a sudden she shot her thunderbolt.

"Are you running away to be married, Ella?" she asked.

A second flush ran over Ella's face, and receded slowly - leaving it very pale. But her head went up rather gallantly.

"No, I ain't," she retorted. "Marriage," she said the words parrot-like, "was made fer th' sort o' folks who can't stick at nothin' unless they're tied. I ain't one of those folks!"

Across the nearly forgotten suit-case, Rose-Marie leaned toward Ella Volsky. Her eyes were suddenly hot with anger.

"Who gave you that sort of an argument?" she demanded. "Who has been filling your head with lies? You never thought of that yourself, Ella - I know you never thought of that yourself!"

Ella's eyes met Rose-Marie's angry glance. Her words, when she spoke, came rapidly - almost tumbled over each other. It was as if some class-resentment, long repressed, were breaking its bounds.

"How d' you know," she demanded passionately, "that I didn't think of that myself? How do you know? You're th' only one, I s'pose," her tone was suddenly mocking, "that knows how t' think! No" - as Rose-Marie started to interrupt - "don't try t' pull any alibi on me! I know th' way you Settlement House *ladies*" - she accented the word - "feel about *us*. You have clubs for us, an' parties, an' uplift meetin's. You pray fer us - an' with us. You tell us who t' marry, an' how t' bring up our children, an' what butcher t' buy our meat off of. But when it comes t' understandin' us - an' likin' us! Well, you're too good, that's all." She paused, staring at Rose-Marie's incredulous face with insolent eyes.

"You're like all th' rest," she went on, after a moment, "just like all th' rest. I was beginnin' t' think that you was diff'rent. You've been so white about Bennie. An' you washed Ma's hair - I wouldn't 'a' done that myself! But now - now it sticks out all over you; th' I'm-better-'n-you-are stuff. I never could think of a thing, *I* couldn't. But you - you're smart, you are. You could think -"

Rose-Marie's cheeks were flushed with a very real resentment, as she interrupted the girl's flow of half-articulate speech.

"Ella," she said, and her words, too, came rapidly, "you know that you're not being fair - you know it! I've never held apart from you in any way. Oh, I realize that we've been brought up in different - surroundings. And it's made us different from each other in the unimportant things. But we're both girls, Ella - we're both young and we've both got all of life before us. And so, perhaps, we can understand each other" - she was fumbling mentally for words, in an effort to make clear her meaning - "more than either of us realize. I wasn't, for one moment, trying to patronize you when I said what I did. I was only wondering how you happened to say something that I wouldn't ever dream of saying - that no nice girl, who had a real under-standing of life" - she wondered, even as she spoke the words, what the Young Doctor would think if he could hear them issuing from her lips - "would dream of saying. You're a nice girl, Ella - or you wouldn't be in the same family with Bennie and Lily. And you're a sensible girl, so you must realize how important and sacred marriage is. Who told you that it was a mistake, Ella? Who," her childish face was very grave, indeed, "who told you such a terrible thing?"

Ella's eyes were blazing - Rose-Marie almost thought that the girl was going to strike her! But the blazing

Margaret E. Sangster

eyes wavered, after a moment, and fell.

"My gentleman fren' says marriage is wrong," said Ella. "He knows a lot. And he has *so* much money" - she made a wide gesture with her hands - "I can have a nice place ter live, Miss Rose-Marie, an' pretty clothes. Lookit Ma; she's married an' she ain't got nothin'! I can have coats an' hats an' -"

Rose-Marie touched Ella's hand, timidly, with her cool fingers.

"But you'll have to pay for them, Ella," she said. "Think, dear; will the coats and hats be worth the price that you'll have to pay? Will they be worth the price of self-respect - will they be worth the price of honourable wifehood and - motherhood? Will the pretty clothes, Ella, make it easier for you to look into the face of some other woman - who has kept straight? Will they?"

Ella raised her eyes and, in their suddenly vague expression, Rose-Marie saw a glimmering of the faded, crushed mother. She hurried on.

"What kind of a chap is this gentleman friend," she raged, "to ask so much of you, dear? Is there - is there any reason why he can't marry you? Is he tied to some one else?"

All at once Ella was sobbing, with gusty, defiant sobs.

"Not as far as I've heard of, there ain't nobody else," she sobbed. "I don't know much about him, Miss Rose-Marie. Jim gimme a knockdown ter him, one night, in a dance-hall. I thought he was all right - Jim said he was ... An' he said he loved me, an'" - wildly - "I love him, too! An' I hate it all, here, except Lily -"

Rose-Marie, thinking rapidly, seized her advantage.

"Will going away with him," she asked steadily, "be worth never seeing Lily again? For you wouldn't be able to see her again - you wouldn't feel able to touch her, you know, if your hands weren't - clean. You bought her a religious picture, Ella, and a flower. Why? Because you know, in your heart, that she's aware of religion and beauty and sweetness! Going away with this man, Ella, will separate you from Lily, just as completely as an ocean - flowing between the two of you - would make a separation! And all of your life you'll have to know that she's suffering some-where, perhaps; that maybe somebody's hurting her - that her dresses are dirty and her hair isn't combed! Every time you hear a little child crying you'll think of Lily - who can't cry aloud. Every time a pair of blue eyes look into your face you'll think of her eyes - that can't see. Will going away with him be worth never knowing, Ella, whether she's alive or dead - "

Ella had stopped sobbing, but the acute misery of her face was somehow more pitiful than tears. Rose-Marie waited, for a moment, and then - as Ella did not speak - she got up from her place beside the suit-case, and going to the dividing door, opened it softly.

The room was as she had left it. Mrs. Volsky was still bending above the tubs, Lily was standing in almost the same place in which she had been left. With hurried steps Rose-Marie crossed the room, and took the child's slim, little hand in her own.

"Come with me, honey," she said, almost forgetting that Lily could not hear her voice. "Come with me," and she led her gently back to the inner room.

Ella was sitting on the floor, her face still wan, her attitude unconsciously tragic. But as the child, clinging to Rose-Marie's hand, came over to her side, she was suddenly galvanized into action.

"Oh, darlin', darlin'," she sobbed wildly, "Ella was a-goin' ter leave you! Ella was a-goin' away. But she isn't now - not now! Darlin'," her arms were flung wildly about the little figure, "show, some way, that you forgive Ella - who loves you!"

Rose-Marie was crying, quite frankly. All at once she dropped down on the floor and put her arms about the two sisters - the big one and the little one - and her sobs mingled with Ella's. But, curiously enough, as she stood like a little statue between them, a sudden smile swept across the face of Lily. She might, almost, have understood.

XIV

PA STEPS ASIDE

They wept together for a long time, Ella and Rose-Marie. And as they cried something grew out of their common emotion. It was a something that they both felt subconsciously - a something warm and friendly. It might have been a new bond of affection, a new chain of love. Rose-Marie, as she felt it, was able to say to herself - with more of tolerance than she had ever known -

"If I had been as tempted and as unhappy as she - well, I might, perhaps, have reacted in the same way!"

And Ella, sobbing in the arms of the girl that she had never quite understood, was able to tell herself: "She's right - dead right! The straight road's the only road...."

It was little Lily who created a diversion. She had been standing, very quietly, in the shelter of their arms for some time - she had a way of standing with an infinite patience, for hours, in one place. But suddenly, as if drawn by some instinct, she dropped down on the floor, beside the cheap suit-case, and her small hands, shaking with eagerness, started to take out the clothes that had been flung into it.

It was uncanny, almost, to see the child so happily beginning to unpack the suit-case. The sight dried Rose-Marie's tears in an almost miraculous way.

"Let's put away the things," she suggested shakily, to Ella. "For you won't be going now, will you?"

The face that Ella Volsky lifted was a changed face. Her expression was a shade more wistful, perhaps, but the somber glow had gone out of her eyes, leaving them softer than Rose-Marie had supposed possible.

"No, Miss," she said quietly, "I won't be going - away. You're right, it ain't worth the price!" And the incident, from that moment, was closed.

They unpacked the garments - there weren't many of them - quietly. But Rose-Marie was very glad, deep in her soul, and she somehow felt that Ella's mind was relieved of a tremendous strain. They didn't speak again, but there was something in the way Ella's hand touched her little sister's sunny hair that was more revealing than words. And there was something in the way Rose-Marie's mouth curved blithely up that told a whole story of satisfaction and content. It seemed as if peace, with her white wings folded and at rest, was hovering, at last, above the Volsky flat.

And then, all at once, the momentary lull was over. All at once the calm was shattered as a china cup, falling from a careless hand, is broken. There was a sudden burst of noise in the front room; of rough words; of a woman sobbing. There was the sound of Mrs. Volsky's voice, raised in an unwonted cry of anguish, there was a trickle of water slithering down upon an uncarpeted floor - as if the wash-tub had been overturned.

It was the final event of an unsettling day - the last straw. Forgetting Lily, forgetting the unpacking, Rose-Marie jumped to her feet, ran to the door. Ella followed. They stood together on the threshold of the outer room, and stared.

The room seemed full of people - shouting, gesticulating people. And in the foreground was Jim - as sleek and well groomed as ever. Of all the crowd he seemed the only one who was composed. In front of him stood Mrs. Volsky - her face drawn and white, her hands clasped in a way that was singularly and primitively appealing.

At first Rose-Marie thought that the commotion had to do with Jim. She was always half expecting to hear that he had been apprehended in some sort of mischief, that he had been accused of some crime. But she dismissed the idea quickly - his composure was too real to be born of bravado. It was while her brain groped for some new solution that she became conscious of Mrs. Volsky's voice.

"Oh, he ain't," the woman was moaning, "say he ain't! My man - he could not be so! There ain't no truth in it - there can't be no truth.... Say as he ain't been done to so bad! Say it!"

Ella, with a movement that was all at once love-filled, stepped quickly to her mother's side. As she faced the crowd - and Jim - her face was also drawn; drawn and apprehensive.

"What's up?" she queried tersely of her brother. "What's up?"

Margaret E. Sangster

The face of Jim was calm and almost smiling as he answered. Behind him the shrill voices of the crowd sounded, like a background, to the blunt words that he spoke.

"Pa was comin' home drunk," he told Ella, "an' he was ran inter by a truck. He was smashed up pretty bad; dead right away, th' cop said. But they took him ter a hospital jus' th' same. Wonder why they'd take a stiff ter a hospital?"

Mrs. Volsky's usually colourless voice was breaking into loud, almost weird lamentation. Ella stood speechless. But Rose-Marie, the horror of it all striking to her very soul, spoke.

"It can't be true," she cried, starting forward and - in the excitement of the moment - laying her hand upon Jim's perfectly tailored coat sleeve. "It can't be true.... It's too terrible!"

Jim's laugh rang out heartlessly, eerily, upon the air.

"It ain't so terrible!" he told Rose-Marie. "Pa - he wasn't no good! He wasn't a reg'lar feller - like me." All at once his well-manicured white hand crept down over her hand. "*He wasn't a reg'lar feller,*" he repeated, "*like me!*"

XV

A SOLUTION

As Rose-Marie left the Volsky flat - Ella had begged her to go; had assured her that it would be better to leave Mrs. Volsky to her inarticulate grief - her brain was in a whirl. Things had happened, in the last few hours, with a kaleidoscopic rapidity - the whirl of events had left her mind in a dazed condition. She told herself, over and over, that Ella was saved. But she found it hard to believe that Ella would ever find happiness, despite her salvation, in the grim tenement that was her home. She told herself that Bennie was learning to travel the right road - that the Scout Club would be the means of leading him to other clubs and that the other clubs would, in time, introduce him to Sunday-school and to the church. She told herself that Mrs. Volsky was willing to try; very willing to try! But of what avail would be Bennie's growing faith and idealism if he had to come, night after night, to the home that was responsible for men like Jim - and like Pa?

Pa! Rose-Marie realized with a new sense of shock that Pa was no longer a force to reckon with. Pa was dead - had been crushed by a truck. Never again would he slouch drunkenly into the flat, never again would he throw soiled clothing and broken bottles and heavy

Margaret E. Sangster

shoes into newly tidied corners. He was dead and he had - after all - been the one link that tied the Volskys to their dingy quarters! With Pa gone the family could seek cleaner, sweeter rooms - rooms that would have been barred to the family of a drunkard! With Pa gone the air would clear, magically, of some of its heaviness.

Rose-Marie, telling herself how much the death of Pa was going to benefit the Volsky family, felt all at once heartless. She had been brought up in an atmosphere where death carries sorrow with it - deep sorrow and sanctity. She remembered the dim parlours of the little town when there was a funeral - she remembered the singing of the village choir and the voice of the pastor, slightly unsteady, perhaps, but very confident of the life hereafter. She remembered the flowers, and the mourners in their black gowns, and the pure tears of grief. She had always seen folk meet death so - meet it rather beautifully.

But the passing of Pa! She shuddered to think of its cold cruelty - it was rather like his life. He had been snuffed out - that was all - snuffed out! There would be for him no dim parlour, no singing choir, no pastor with an unsteady voice. The black-robed mourners would be absent, and so would the flowers. His going would cause not a ripple in the life of the community - it would bring with it better opportunities for his family, rather than a burden of sorrow!

"I can't grieve for him!" Rose-Marie told herself desperately. "I can't grieve for him! It's the only chance he ever gave to his children - *dying*! Perhaps, without him, they'll be able to make good...."

She was crossing the park - splashed with sunshine, it was. And suddenly she remembered the first time that she had met Bennie in the park. It seemed centuries away, that first meeting! She remembered how she had been afraid, then, of the crowds. Now she walked through them with a certain assurance - *she belonged.* She had come a long distance since that first meeting with Bennie - a very long distance! She told herself that she had proved her ability to cope with circumstance - had proved her worth, almost. Why, now, should the Superintendent keep her always in the shadow of the Settlement House - why should the Young Doctor laugh at her desire to help people? She had something to show them - she could flaunt Bennie before their eyes, she could quote the case of Ella; she could produce Mrs. Volsky, broken of spirit but ready to do anything that she could. And - last but not least - she would show Lily to them, Lily who had been hidden away from the eyes of the ones who could help her - Lily who so desperately needed help!

All at once Rose-Marie was weary of deceit. She would be glad - ever so glad - to tell her story to the Superintendent! She was tired of going out furtively of an afternoon to help these folk that she had come to help. She wanted to go in an open way - with the stamp of approval upon her. The Superintendent had said, once, that she would hardly be convincing to the people of the slums. With the Volsky family to show, she could prove that she had been convincing, very convincing!

With a singing heart she approached the Settlement House. With a smile on her lips she went up the brownstone steps, pushed wide the door - which was never locked. And then she hurried, as fast as her feet could hurry, to the Superintendent's tiny office.

The Superintendent was in. She answered Rose-Marie's knock with a cheery word, but, when the girl entered the room, she saw that the Superintendent's kind eyes were troubled.

"What's the matter?" she questioned, forgetting, for a moment, the business of which she had been so full. "What's the matter? You look ever so worried!"

The Superintendent's tired face broke into a smile.

"Was I looking as woe-begone as that?" she queried. "I didn't realize that I was. Nothing serious is the matter, dear - nothing very serious! Only Katie's sister in the old country is ill - and Katie is going home to stay with her. And it's just about impossible to get a good maid, nowadays - it seems as if Katie has been with me for a lifetime. I expect that we'll manage, somehow, but I don't just fancy cooking and sweeping, and running the Settlement House, too!"

All at once an idea leaped, full-blown, into the brain of Rose-Marie. She leaned forward and laid her hand upon the Superintendent's arm.

"I wonder," she asked excitedly, "if you'd consider a woman with a family to take Katie's place? The family isn't large - just a small boy who goes to school, and a small girl, and an older girl who is working. There's a grown son, but he can take care of himself..." the last she said almost under her breath. "He can take care of himself. It would be better, for them -"

The Superintendent was eyeing Rose-Marie curiously.

"We have plenty of sleeping-rooms on the top floor," she said slowly, "and I suppose that the older girl could help a bit, evenings. Why, yes, perhaps a family might solve the problem - it's easier to keep a woman with children than one who is," she laughed, "heart-whole and fancy free! Who are they, dear, and how do you happen to know of them?"

Rose-Marie sat down, suddenly, in a chair beside the Superintendent's desk. All at once her knees were shaky - all at once she felt strangely apprehensive.

"Once," she began, and her voice quivered slightly, "I met a little boy, in the park. He was hurting a kitten. I started to scold him and then something made me question him, instead. And I found out that he was hurting the kitten because he didn't know any better - think of it, *because he didn't know any better*! And so I was interested, ever so interested. And I decided it was my duty to know something of him - to find out what sort of an environment was responsible for him."

The Superintendent's tired face was alight She leaned forward to ask a question.

"How long ago," she questioned, "did you meet this child, in the park?"

Rose-Marie flushed. The time, suddenly, seemed very long to her.

"It was the day that I came home bringing a little gray cat with me," she said. "It was the day that I quarreled with Dr. Blanchard at the luncheon table. Do you remember?"

The Superintendent smiled reminiscently. "Ah, yes, I remember!" she said. And then - "Go on with the story, dear."

Rose-Marie went on.

"I found the place where he lived," she said hurriedly. "Yes - I know that you wouldn't have let me go if you'd known about it! That's why I didn't tell you. I found the place where he lived; an unspeakable tenement on an unspeakable street. And I met, there, his family - a most remarkable family! There was a mother, and an older sister, and an older brother, and a drunken father, and a little crippled girl...."

And then, shaking inwardly, Rose-Marie told the story of the Volskys. She told it well; better than she realized. For the Superintendent's eyes never left her face and - at certain parts of the story - the Superintendent's cheeks grew girlishly pink. She told of the saving of Ella - she told of Bennie, explaining that he was the same child whom the Young Doctor had met in the hall. She told of Mrs. Volsky's effort to better herself, and of Jim's snake-like smoothness. And then she told of Lily - Lily with her almost unearthly beauty and her piteous physical condition. As she told of Lily the Superintendent's kind eyes filled with tears, and her lips quivered.

"Oh," she breathed, "if only something could be done for her - if only something could be done! Billy Blanchard must see her at once - he's done marvellous things with the crippled children of the neighbourhood!"

With a feeling of sudden confidence Rose-Marie

smiled. She realized that she had caught the Superintendent's interest - and her sympathy. It would be easier, now, to give the family their chance! Her voice was more calm as she went on with the narrative. It was only when she told of the death of Pa that her lips trembled.

"You'll think that I'm hard and callous," she said, "taking his death so easily. But I can't help feeling that it's for the best. They could never have broken away - not with him alive. *You* would never have taken them in - if he had had to be included! You couldn't have done it.... But now," her voice was aquiver with eagerness, "now, say that they may come! Say that Mrs. Volsky may take Katie's place. Oh, I know that she isn't very neat; that she doesn't cook as we would want her to. But she can learn and, free from the influence of her husband and son, I'm sure she'll change amazingly. Say that you'll give the family a chance!"

The Superintendent was wavering. "I'm not so sure," she began, and hesitated. "I'm not so sure - "

Rose-Marie interrupted. Her voice was very soft.

"It will mean," she said, "that Lily will be here, under the doctor's care. It will mean that she will get well - perhaps! For her sake give them a chance...."

The Superintendent's eyes were fixed upon space. When she spoke, she spoke irrelevantly.

"Then," she said, "that was where you went every afternoon - to the tenement. You weren't out with some man, after all?"

Rose-Marie hung her head. "I went to the tenement every afternoon," she admitted, "to the *tenement*. Oh, I know that you're angry with me - I know it. And I don't in the least blame you. I've been deceitful, I've *sneaked* away when your back was turned, I've practically told lies to you! Don't think," her voice was all a-tremble, "don't think that I haven't been sorry. I've been tremendously sorry ever so many times. I've tried to tell you, too - often. And I've tried to make you think my way. Do you remember the talk we had, that night when we were both so tired, in your sitting-room - before Dr. Blanchard came? I was trying to scrape up the courage to tell you, then, but you so disagreed with me that I didn't dare!"

The Superintendent seemed scarcely to be listening. There seemed to be something upon her mind.

"Rose-Marie," she said with a mock sternness, "you're evading my questions. Answer me, child! Isn't there any one that you - care for? Weren't you out with some man?"

Rose-Marie was blushing furiously.

"No," she admitted, "I wasn't out with a man. I never had any sort of a sweetheart, not ever! I just let you all think that I was with some one because - if I hadn't let you think that way - you might have made me stay in. I wouldn't have made a point of deliberately telling you a falsehood - but Dr. Blanchard gave me the idea and " - defiantly - "I just let him think what he wanted to think!"

The Superintendent was laughing.

"What he *wanted* to think!" she exclaimed. "Oh, Rose-Marie - you've a lot to answer for! What he wanted to think...." Suddenly the laugh died out of her voice, all at once she was very serious. "Perhaps," she said slowly, "your idea about the Volsky family is a good one. We'll try it out, dear! There was a MAN, once, Who said: 'Suffer the little children to come - 'Why, Rose-Marie, what's the matter?" For Rose-Marie, her face hidden in the crook of her elbow, was crying like a very tired child.

Margaret E. Sangster

XVI

ENTER - JIM

It was with a light heart that Rose-Marie started back to the tenement. The tears had cleared her soul of the months of evasion that had so worried her - she felt suddenly free and young and happy. It was as if a rainbow had come up, tenderly, out of a storm-tossed sky; it was as if a star was shining, all at once, through the blackness of midnight. She felt a glad assurance of the future - a faith in the Hand of God, stretched out to His children. "Everything," she sing-songed, joyously, to herself, "will come right, now. Everything will come right!"

It was strange how she suddenly loved all of the people, the almost mongrel races of people, who thronged the streets! She smiled brightly at a mother, pushing a baby-buggy - she thrust a coin into the withered hand of an old beggar. On a crowded corner she paused to listen to the vague carollings of a barrel organ, to pat the head of a frayed looking little monkey that hopped about in time to the music. All at once she wanted to know a dozen foreign languages so that she could tell those who passed her by that she was their friend - *their friend!*

And yet, despite her sudden feeling of kinship to these

people of the slums, she did not loiter. For she was the bearer of a message, a message of hope! She wished, as she sped through the crowded streets, that her feet were winged so that she might hurry the faster! She wanted to see the expression of bewilderment on Mrs. Volsky's face, she wanted to see a light dawn in Ella's great eyes, she wanted to whisper a message of - of life, almost - into Lily's tiny useless ear. And, most of all, she wanted to feel Bennie's warm, grubby little fingers touching her hand! Jim - she hoped that Jim would be out when she arrived. She did not want to have Jim throw cold water upon her plans - which did not include him. Well she knew that the arrangement would make no real difference to him - it was not love of family that kept him from leaving the dirty, crowded little flat. It was the protection of a family, with its pseudo-respectability, that he wanted. It was the locked room, which no one would think of prying into, that he desired.

She went in through the mouth-like tenement door - it was no longer frightful to her - with a feeling of intense emotion. She climbed the narrow stairs, all five flights of them, with never a pause for breath. And then she was standing, once again, in front of the Volskys' door. She knocked, softly.

Everything was apparently very still in the Volsky flat. All up and down the hall came the usual sounds of the house; the stairs echoed with noise. But behind the closed door silence reigned supreme. As Rose-Marie stood there she felt a strange mental chill - the chill of her first doubt. Perhaps the Volskys would not want to come with her to the Settlement House, perhaps they would resent her attitude - would call it interference. Perhaps they would tell her that they were tired of her -

and of her plans. Perhaps - But the door, swinging open, cut short her suppositions.

Jim stood in the doorway. He was in his shirt sleeves but - even divested of his coat - he was still too painfully immaculate - too well groomed. Rose-Marie, looking at him, felt a sudden primitive desire to see him dirty and mussed up. She wished, and the wish surprised her, that she might sometime see him with his hair rumpled, his collar torn, his eye blackened and - she could hardly suppress a hysterical desire to laugh as the thought struck her - his nose bleeding. Somehow his smooth, hard neatness was more offensive to her than his mother's dirty apron - than his small brother's frankly grimy hands. She spoke to him in a cool little voice that belied her inward disturbance.

"Where," she questioned, "are your mother and Ella? I want to see them."

With a movement that was not ungraceful Jim flung wide the door. Indeed, Rose-Marie told herself, as she stepped into the Volsky flat, Jim was never ungraceful. There was something lithe and cat-like in his slightest movement, just as there was something feline in the expression of his eyes. Rose-Marie often felt like a small, helpless mouse when Jim was staring at her.

"Where are your mother and Ella?" she questioned again as she stepped into the room. "I *do* want to see them!"

Jim was dragging forward a chair. He answered.

"Then yer'd better sit down 'n' make yourself at home," he told her, "fer they've gone out. They're down t' th' hospital, now, takin' a last slant at Pa. Ma's cryin' to beat th' band - you'd think that she really liked *him*! An' Ella's cryin', too - she's fergot how he uster whip her wit' a strap when she was a kid! An' they've took Bennie; Bennie ain't cryin' but he's a-holdin' to Ma's hand like a baby. Oh," he laughed sneeringly, "it's one grand little family group that they make!"

Rose-Marie sat down gingerly upon the edge of the chair. She did not relish the prospect of spending any time alone with Jim, but a certain feeling of pride kept her from leaving the place. She would not let Jim know that she feared him - it would flatter him to think that he had so much influence over her. She would stay, even though the staying made her uneasy! But she hoped, from the bottom of her heart, that the rest of the family would not be long at the hospital.

"When did they go out?" she questioned, trying to make her tone casual. "Do you expect them back soon?"

Jim sat down in a chair that was near her own. He leaned forward as he answered.

"They haven't been gone so awful long," he told her. "An' - say - what's th' difference *when* they gets back? I never have no chance to talk wit' you - not ever! An'," he sighed with mock tragedy, "an' I have so much t' say t' yer! You never have a word fer me - think o' that! An' think o' all th' time yer waste on Bennie - an' him too young t' know a pretty girl when he sees one!"

Rose-Marie flushed and hated herself for doing it. "We'll leave personalities out of this!" she said primly.

Jim was laughing, but there was a sinister note in his mirth.

"Not much we won't!" he told her. "I like you - see? You're th' best lookin' girl in this neck o' woods - even if you do live at the Settlement House! If you'd learn to dress more snappy - t' care more about hats than yer do about Bible Classes - you'd make a big hit when yer walked out on Delancy Street. There ain't a feller livin' as wouldn't turn t' look at yer - not one! Say, kid," he leaned still closer, "I'm strong fer yer when yer cheeks get all pink-like. I'm strong fer yer any time a-tall!"

Rose-Marie was more genuinely shocked than she had ever been in her life. The flush receded slowly from her face.

"You'd like me to be more interested in clothes than in Bible Classes!" she said slowly. "You'd like me to go parading down Delancy Street ..." she paused, and then - "You're a fine sort of a man," she said bitterly - "a fine sort of a man! Oh, I know. I know the sort of people you introduce to Ella - and she's your sister. I've seen the way you look at Lily, and she's your sister, too! You wouldn't think of making things easier for your mother; and you'd give Bennie a push down - instead of a boost *up*! And you scoff at your father - lying dead in his coffin! You're a fine sort of a *man*.... I don't believe that you've a shred of human affection in your whole make-up!"

Jim had risen slowly to his feet. There was no anger in his face - only a huge amusement. Rose-Marie, watching his expression, knew all at once that nothing she said would have the slightest effect upon him. His sensibilities were too well concealed, beneath a tough veneer of conceit, to be wounded. His soul seemed too well hidden to be reached.

"So that's what you think, is it?" he asked, and his voice was almost silky, it was so smooth, "so that's what you think! I haven't any 'human affection in my make-up,'" he was imitating her angry voice, "I haven't any 'human affection'!" he laughed suddenly, and bent with a swift movement until his face was on a level with her face. "Lot yer know about it!" he told her and his voice thickened, all at once, "lot yer know about it! I'm crazy about you, little kid - just crazy! Yer th' only girl as I've ever wanted t' tie up to, get that? How'd yer like t' marry me?"

For one sickening moment Rose-Marie thought that she had misunderstood. And then she saw his face and knew that he had been deadly serious. Her hands fluttered up until they rested, like frightened birds, above her heart.

XVII

AN ANSWER

There was eagerness - and a hint of something else - in Jim's voice as he repeated his question.

"Well," he asked for the second time, "what d' yer say about it - huh? How'd yer like ter marry me?"

Rose-Marie's fascinated eyes were on his face. At the first she had hardly believed her ears - but her ears had evidently been functioning properly. Jim wanted to marry her - to marry *her*! It was a possibility that she had never dreamed of - a thought that she had never, for one moment, entertained. Jim had always seemed so utterly of another world - of another epoch, almost. He spoke a language that was far removed from her language, his mind worked differently - even his emotions were different from her emotions. He might have been living upon another planet - so distant he had always seemed from her. *And yet he had asked her to marry him*!

Like every other normal girl, Rose-Marie had thought ahead to the time when she would have a home and a husband. She had dreamed of the day when her knight would come riding - a visionary, idealized figure, always, but a noble one! She had pictured a hearth-fire, and a blue and white kitchen with aluminum pans and glass baking dishes. She had even wondered how tiny fingers would feel as they curled about her hand - if a wee head would be heavy upon her breast.

Of late her dreams, for some reason, had become a little less misty - a little more definite. The figure of her knight had been a trifle more clear cut - the armour of her imagination had given place to rough tweed suits and soft felt hats. And the children had looked at her, from out of the shadows, with wide, dark eyes - almost like real children. Her thoughts had shaped themselves about a figure that was not the romantic creation of girlhood - that was strong and willing and very tender. Dr. Blanchard - had he not been mistaken upon so many subjects - would have fitted nicely into the picture!

But Jim - of all people, *Jim!* He was as far removed from the boundaries of her dream as the North Pole is removed from the South. His patent leather hair - she could not picture it against her arm - his mouth, thin-lipped and too red.... She shuddered involuntarily, as she thought of it and the man, bending above her, saw the shudder.

"Well," he questioned for the third time, "what about it? I'm a reg'lar guy, ain't I? How'd you like to marry me?"

Rose-Marie moistened her lips before she answered. Her voice, when it came, was very husky.

"Why, Jim," she said faintly, "what an idea! How did you ever come to think of it?"

The man's face was flushed. His words tumbled, quickly, from his unsteady mouth.

"I'm crazy about yer, kid," he said, "crazy about yer! Don't think that bein' married t' me will mean as you'll have ter live in a dump like this-there" - the sweep of his arm was expressive - "fer yer won't! You'll have th' grandest flat in this city - anywhere yer say'll suit me! Yer'll have hats an' dresses, an' a car - if yer want it. Yer'll have everything - if yer'll marry me! What d' yer say?"

Rose-Marie's face was a study of mixed emotions - consternation struggling with incredulity for first place. The man saw the unbelief; for he hurried on before she could speak.

"Yer think that I'm like my pa was" - he told her - "livin' on measly wages! Well, I ain't. Some nights I make a pile that runs inter thousands - an' it'll be all fer yer! All fer yer!"

Of a sudden, Rose-Marie spoke. She was scarcely tactful.

"How do you make all of this money, Jim?" she questioned; "do you come by it honestly?"

A dark wave of colour spread over the man's face - dyeing it to an ugly crimson.

"What's it matter how I get it," he snarled, "long's I get it! What business is it of yers how I come by my coin? I ain't stagin' a investergation. And" - his face softened suddenly, "an' yer wouldn't understand, anyhow! Yer only a girl - a little kid! What's it matter how I gets th' roll - long as I'm willin' ter spend it on m' sweetie? What's it matter?" He made a movement as if to take her into his arms - "*What's it matter?*" he questioned again.

Like a flash Rose-Marie was upon her feet. With a swing of her body she had evaded his arms. Her face was white and drawn, but her mind was exceptionally active - more active than it had ever been in all of her life. She knew that Jim was in a difficult mood - that a word, one way or the other, would make him as easy to manage as a kitten or as relentless as a panther, stalking his prey. She knew that it was in her power to say the word that would calm him until the return of his mother and his sister. And yet she found it well-nigh impossible to say that word.

"I'm tired of deceit," she told herself, as she stepped back in the direction of the door. "I'll not say anything to him that isn't true! ... Nothing can happen to me, anyway," she assured herself. "This is the twentieth century, and I'm Rose-Marie Thompson. This is a civilized country - nothing can hurt me! I'm not afraid - not while God is taking care of me!"

Jim had straightened up. He seemed, suddenly, to tower.

"Well," he growled, "how about it? When'll we be married?"

Rose-Marie raised her head gallantly.

"We won't ever be married, Jim Volsky!" she told him, and even to her own surprise there was not the sugges-tion of a quaver in her voice. "We won't ever be married. I'm surprised at you for suggesting it!"

The man stared at her, a moment, and his eyes showed clearly that he did not quite understand.

"Yer mean," he stammered at last, "that yer t'rowing me down?"

Rose-Marie's head was still gallantly lifted.

"I mean," she said, "that I won't marry you! Please - we'll let the matter drop, at once!"

The man came a step nearer. The bewilderment was dying from his face.

"Not much, we won't let the matter drop!" he snarled. "What's yer reason fer turnin' me down - huh?"

It was then that Rose-Marie made her mistake. It was then that she ceased to be tactful. But suddenly she was tired, desperately tired, of Jim's persistence. Suddenly she was too tired even to be afraid. The lift of her chin was very proud - proud with some ingrained pride of race, as she answered. Behind her stood a long line of ancestors with gentle blood, ancestors who had known the meaning of chivalry.

Coolly she surveyed him. Dispassionately she noticed the lack of breeding in his face, the marks of early dissipation, the lines that sin had etched. And as she looked she laughed with just the suggestion of hauteur. For the first time in her life Rose-Marie was experiencing a touch of snobbishness, of class distinction.

"We won't discuss my reason," she told him slowly; "it should be quite evident to *any one*!"

Not many weeks before, Rose-Marie had told the Young Doctor - in the presence of the Superintendent - that she loved the people of the slums. She had been so sure of herself then - so certain that she spoke the truth. More recently she had assured the Superintendent that she could cope with any situation. And that very afternoon she had told Ella that they were alike, were just young girls - both of them - with all of life in front of them, with the same hopes and the same fears and the same ambitions.

She had believed the statement that she had made, so emphatically, to the Young Doctor - she had believed it very strongly. She had been utterly sure of herself when she begged the Superintendent to let her know more of life. And, during her talk with Ella, she had felt a real kinship to the whole of the Volsky family! But now that she had come face to face with a crisis - now that she was meeting her big test - she knew that her strong beliefs were weakening and that she was no longer at all sure of herself! And as for being kin to the Volskys - the idea was quite unthinkable.

Always, Rose-Marie had imagined that a proposal of marriage would be the greatest compliment that a man could pay a girl. But the proposal of the man in front of her did not seem in the least complimentary. She realized - with the only feeling of irony she had ever known, that this proposal was her very first. And she was looking upon it as an insult. With a tiny curl of her lips she raised her eyes until they met Jim's eyes.

"It should be quite evident," she repeated, "to

any one!"

Jim Volsky's face had turned to a dark mottled red. His slim, well manicured hands were clenched at his sides.

"Y' mean," he questioned, and his voice had an ugly ring, "y' mean I ain't good enough fer yer?"

All at once the snobbishness had slipped, like a worn coat, from the shoulders of the girl. She was Rose-Marie Thompson again - Settlement worker. She was no better, despite the ancestors with gentle blood, than the man in front of her - just more fortunate. She realized that she had been not only unkind, but foolish. She tried, hurriedly - and with a great scare looking out of her wide eyes - to repair the mistake that she had made.

"I don't mean that I am better than you, Jim," she said softly, "not in the matter of family. We are all the children of God - we are all brothers and sisters in His sight."

Jim Volsky interrupted. He came nearer to Rose-Marie - so near that only a few inches of floor space lay between them.

"Don't yer go sayin' over Sunday-school lessons at me," he snarled. "I know what yer meant. Yer think I ain't good enough - t' marry yer. Well" - he laughed shortly, "well, maybe I ain't good enough - t' marry yer! But I guess I'm good enough t' kiss yer - " All at once his hands shot out, closed with the strength of a vise upon her arms, just above her elbows. "I guess I'm good enough t' kiss yer!" he repeated gloatingly.

Rose-Marie felt cold fear creeping through her veins. There was something clammy in Jim's touch, something more than menacing in his eyes. She knew that her strength was nothing to be pitted against his - she knew that in any sort of a struggle she would be easily subdued. And yet she knew that she would rather die than feel his lips upon hers. She felt an intense loathing for him - the loathing that some women feel for toads and lizards.

"Jim," she said slowly and distinctly, "let go of me *this instant*!"

The man was bending closer. A thick lock of his heavy hair had shaken down over his forehead, giving him a strangely piratical look.

"Not much I won't," he told her. "*So I ain't good enough -*"

All at once Rose-Marie felt the blindness of rage - unreasoning, deadly anger. Only two things she knew - that she hated Jim and that she would not let him kiss her. She spoke sudden defiant words that surprised even herself.

"No," she told him, and her voice was hysterically high, "no, you're not good enough! You're not good enough for *any* decent girl! You're bad - too bad to lay your fingers upon me. You're - you're unclean! Let go of me or I'll" - her courage was oozing rapidly away, "or I'll *scream*!"

Jim Volsky's too red lips were on a level with her own. His voice came thickly. "Scream, if you want to, little kid!" he said. "Scream t' beat th' band! There ain't no one t' hear yer. Ma an' Ella an' Bennie are at the hospital - givin' Pa th' once over. An' th' folks in this house are used t' yellin'. They'd oughter be! Scream if yer want to - but I'm a-goin' ter have my kiss!"

Rose-Marie could feel the warmth of his breath upon her face. Knowing the futility - the uselessness of it - she began to struggle. Desperately she tried to twist her arms from the slim, brutal hands that held them - but the hands did not loosen their hold. She told herself, as she struggled, that Jim had spoken the truth - that a scream, more or less, was an every-day occurrence in the tenement.

All at once she realized, with a dazed, sinking feeling, that the Young Doctor had had some foundation of truth in certain of his statements. Some of the slum people were like animals - very like animals! Jim was all animal as he bent above her - easily holding her with his hands. Nothing that she said could reach him - nothing. She realized why the Young Doctor had wanted her to leave the Settlement House before any of her dreams had been shattered, before her faith in mankind had been abused! She realized why, at times, he had hurt her, and with the realization came the knowledge that she wanted him, desperately, at that minute - that he, out of all the people in the world, was the one that her heart was calling to in her time of need. She wanted his strength, his protection.

Once before, earlier in the afternoon, she had realized that there was much of the cat in Jim. Now she realized it again, with a new sense of fear and dislike. For Jim was not claiming the kiss that he wanted, in a straight-forward way - he was holding her gloatingly, as a cat tortures a mouse. He was letting her know, without words, that she was utterly helpless - that he could kiss her when he wanted to, and not until he wanted to. There was something horribly playful in his attitude. She struggled again - but more weakly, her strength was going. If there were only somebody to help - somebody!

And then, all at once, she remembered - with a blinding sense of relief - what she had been forgetting. She remembered that there was Somebody - a Somebody Who is always ready to help - a Somebody who watches over the fate of every little sparrow.

"If you hurt me," she said desperately, to Jim, "God will know! Let go of me - or I'll -"

Jim interrupted.

"Yer'll scream!" he chuckled, and there was cruel mirth in the chuckle. "Yer'll scream, an' God will take care o' yer! Well - scream! I don't believe as God can help yer. God ain't never been in this tenement - as far as I know!"

Despite her weight of fear and loathing, Rose-Marie was suddenly sorry for Jim. There was something pitiful - something of which he did not realize the pathos - in his speech. God had never been in the tenement - *God had never been in the tenement*! All at once she realized that Jim's wickedness, that Jim's point of view, was not wholly his fault. Jim had not been brought up, as she had, in the clean out-of-doors; he - like many another slum child - had grown to manhood without his proper heritage of fresh air and sunshine. One could not entirely blame him for thinking of his home - the only home that he had ever known - as a Godless place. She stopped struggling and her voice was suddenly calm and sweet as she answered Jim's statement.

"God," she said slowly, "*is* in this tenement. God is everywhere, Jim - everywhere! If I call on Him, He will help me!"

All at once Jim had swung her away from him, until he was holding her at arm's length. He looked at her, from between narrowed lids, and there was bitter sarcasm in his eyes.

"Call on Him, then," he taunted, "call on Him! Lotta good it'll do yer!" The very tone of his voice was a sacrilege, as he said it.

Rose-Marie's eyes were blurred with tears as she spoke her answer to his challenge. She was remembering the prayers that she had said back home - in the little town. She was remembering how her aunts had taught her, when she was a wee girl, to talk with God - to call upon Him in times of deep perplexity. She had called upon Him, often, but she had never really needed Him as she did now. "Help me, God!" she said softly, "*Help me, God*!"

The Volsky flat was still, for a moment. And then, with surprising quickness, the door to the inner room swung open. Jim, who was standing with his back to the door, did not see the tiny, golden-haired figure that stood in the opening, but Rose-Marie caught her breath in a kind of a sob.

"I had forgotten Lily - " she murmured, almost to herself.

Jim, hearing her words, glanced quickly back over his shoulder. And then he laughed, and there was an added brutality in the tone of his laughter.

"Oh - Lily!" he laughed. "Lily! She won't help yer - not much! I was sort of expectin' this God that yer talk about -" The laughter died out of his face and he jerked her suddenly close - so close that she lay trembling in his arms. "Lily can't hear," he exulted, "'r see, 'r speak. *I'll take my kiss - now!*"

It was then that Rose-Marie, forgetting herself in the panic of the moment, screamed. She screamed lustily, twisting her face away from his lips. And as she screamed Lily, as silently as a little wraith, started across the room. She might almost have heard, so straight she came. She might almost have known what was happening, so directly she ran to the spot where Rose-Marie was struggling in the arms of Jim. All at once her thin little hands had fastened themselves upon the man's trouser leg, all at once she was pulling at him, with every bit of her feeble strength.

Rose-Marie, still struggling, felt an added weight of apprehension. Not only her own safety was at stake - Lily, who was so weak, was in danger of being hurt. She jerked back, with another cry.

"Oh, God help me!" she cried, "God help *us*!"

Silently, but with a curious persistence, the child clung to the man's trouser leg. With an oath he looked back again over his shoulder.

"Leave go of me," he mouthed. "Leave go o' me - y' little brat! 'r I'll -"

And "Let go of him, Lily," sobbed Rose-Marie, forgetting that the child could not hear. "Let go of him, or he'll hurt you!"

The child lifted her sightless blue eyes wistfully to the faces above her - the faces that she could not see. And she clung the closer.

Jim was swearing, steadily - swearing with a dogged, horrible regularity. Of a sudden he raised his heavy foot and kicked viciously at the child who clung so tenaciously to his other leg. Rose-Marie, powerless to help, closed her eyes - and opened them again almost spasmodically.

"You brute," she screamed, "*you utter brute!*"

Lily, who had never, in all of her broken little life, felt an unkind touch, wavered, as the man's boot touched her slight body. Her sightless eyes clouded, all at once, with tears. And then, with a sudden piercing shriek, she crumpled up - in a white little heap - upon the floor.

XVIII

AND A MIRACLE

For a moment Rose-Marie was stunned by the child's unexpected cry. She hung speechless, filled with wonderment, in Jim's arms. And then, with a wrench, she was free - was running across the floor to the little huddled bundle that was Lily.

"You beast," she flung back, over her shoulder, as she ran. "You beast! You've killed her!"

Jim did not attempt to follow - or to answer. He had wheeled about, and his face was very pale.

"God!" he said, in a tense whisper, "*God*!" It was the first time that the word, upon his lips, was neither mocking nor profane.

Rose-Marie, with tender hands, gathered the child up from the hard floor. She was not thinking of the miracle that had taken place - she was not thinking of the sound that had come, so unexpectedly, from dumb lips. She only knew that the child was unconscious, perhaps dying. Her trembling fingers felt of the slim wrist; felt almost with apprehension. She was surprised to feel that the pulse was still beating, though faintly.

Margaret E. Sangster

"Get somebody," she said, tersely, to Jim. "Get somebody who knows - something!"

Jim's face was still the colour of ashes. He did not stir - did not seem to have the power to stir.

"Did yer hear her?" he mouthed thickly. "She *yelled*. I heard her. Did yer hear -"

Rose-Marie was holding Lily close to her breast. Her stern young eyes looked across the drooping golden head into the scared face of the man.

"It was God, speaking through her," she said. "It was God. And you - you had denied Him - *you beast*!"

All at once Jim was down upon the floor beside her. The mask of passion had slipped from his face - his shoulders seemed suddenly more narrow - his cruel hands almost futile. Rose-Marie wondered, subconsciously, how she had ever feared him.

"She yelled," he reiterated, "*did yer hear her* -"

Rose-Marie clutched the child tighter in her arms.

"Get some one, at once," she ordered, "if you don't want her to die - if you don't want to be a murderer!"

But Jim had not heard her voice. He was sobbing, gustily.

"I'm t'rough," he was sobbing, "t'rough! Oh - God, fergive -"

It was then that the door opened. And Rose-Marie,

raising eyes abrim with relief, saw that Ella and Mrs. Volsky and Bennie stood upon the threshold.

"What's a-matter?" questioned Mrs. Volsky - her voice sodden with grief. "What's been a-happenin'?" But Ella ran across the space between them, and knelt in front of Rose-Marie.

"Give 'er t' me!" she breathed fiercely; "she's my sister. Give 'er t' me!"

Silently Rose-Marie handed over the light little figure. But as Ella pillowed the dishevelled head upon her shoulder, she spoke directly to Bennie.

"Run to the Settlement House, as fast as ever you can!" she told him. "And bring Dr. Blanchard back with you. Hurry, dear - it may mean Lily's life!" And Bennie, with his grimy face tear-streaked, was out of the door and clattering down the stairs before she had finished.

Ella, her mouth agonized and drawn, was the first to speak after Bennie left the room. When she did speak she asked a question.

"Who done this t' her?" she questioned. "*Who done it*?"

Rose-Marie hesitated. She could feel the eyes of Mrs. Volsky, dumb with suffering, upon her - she could feel Jim's rat-like gaze fixed, with a certain appeal, on her face. At last she spoke.

"Jim will tell you!" she said.

If she had expected the man to evade the issue - if she had expected a downright falsehood from him - she was surprised. For Jim's head came up, suddenly, and his eyes met the burning dark ones of his sister.

"I done it," he said, simply, and he scrambled up from the floor, as he spoke. "I kicked her. She come in when I was tryin' t' kiss" - his finger indicated Rose-Marie, "*her*. Lily got in th' way. So I kicked out hard - then - she," he gulped back a shudder, "she *yelled*!"

Ella was suddenly galvanized into action. She was on her feet, with one lithe, pantherlike movement - the child held tight in her arms.

"Yer kicked her," she said softly - and the gentleness of her voice was ominous. "Yer kicked her! An' she yelled - " For the first time the full significance of it struck her. "*She yelled*?" she questioned, whirling to Rose-Marie; "yer don't mean as she made a *sound*?"

Rose-Marie nodded dumbly. It was Jim's voice that went on with the story.

"She ain't dead," he told Ella, piteously. "She ain't dead. An' - I promise yer true - I'll never do such a thing again. I promise yer true!"

Ella took a step toward him. Her face was suddenly lined, and old. "If she dies," she told him, "*if she dies...*" she hesitated, and then - "Much yer promises mean," she shrilled, "much yer promises -"

Rose-Marie had been watching Jim's face. Almost without meaning to she interrupted Ella's flow of speech.

"I think that he means what he says," she told Ella

slowly. "I think that he means ... what he says."

For she had seen the birth of something - *that might have been soul* - in Jim's haggard eyes.

The child in Ella's arms stirred, weakly, and was still again. But the movement, slight as it was, made the girl forget her brother. Her dark head bent above the fair one.

"Honey," she whispered, "yer goin' ter get well fer Ella - ain't yer? Yer goin' ter get well -"

The door swung open with a startling suddenness, and Rose-Marie sprang forward, her hands outstretched. Framed in the battered wood stood Bennie - the tears streaking his face - and behind him was the Young Doctor. So tall he seemed, so capable, so strong, standing there, that Rose-Marie felt as if her troubles had been lifted, magically, from her shoulders. All at once she ceased to be afraid - ceased to question the ways of the Almighty. All at once she felt that Lily would get better - that the Volskys would be saved to a better life. And all at once she knew something else. And the consciousness of it looked from her wide eyes.

"You!" she breathed. "*You!*"

And, though she had sent for him, herself, she felt a glad sort of surprise surging through her heart.

The Young Doctor's glance, in her direction, was eloquent. But as his eyes saw the child in Ella's arms his expression became impersonal, again, concentrated, and alert. With one stride he reached Ella's side, and took the tiny figure from her arms.

"What's the matter here?" he questioned sharply.

Rose-Marie was not conscious of the words that she used as she described Lily's accident. She glossed over Jim's part in it as lightly as possible; she told, as quickly as she could, the history of the child. And as she told it, the doctor's lean capable hands were passing, with practiced skill, over the little relaxed body. When she told of the child's deaf and dumb condition she was conscious of his absolute attention - though he did not for a moment stop his work - when she spoke of the scream she saw his start of surprise. But his only words were in the nature of commands. "Bring water" - he ordered, "clean water, in a basin. A *clean* basin. Bring a sponge" - he corrected himself - "a clean rag will do - only it must be *clean*" - this to Mrs. Volsky, "you *understand?* Where," his eyes were on Ella's face, "can we lay the child? Is there a *clean* bed, anywhere?"

Ella was shaking with nervousness as she opened the door of the inner room that she and Lily shared. Mrs. Volsky, carrying the basin of water, was sobbing. Jim, standing in the center of the room, was like a statue - only his haunted eyes were alive. The Young Doctor, glancing from face to face, spoke suddenly to Rose-Marie.

"I hate to ask you," he said simply, "but you seem to be the only one who hasn't gone to pieces. Will you come in here with me?"

Rose-Marie nodded, and she spoke, very softly. "Then you think that I'll be able - to help?" she questioned.

The Young Doctor was remembering - or forgetting -

many things.

"I know that you will!" he said, and he spoke as softly as she had done. "I know that you will!"

They went, together, with Lily, into the inner room. And as the Young Doctor closed the door, Rose-Marie knew a very real throb of triumph. For he had admitted that her help was to be desired - that she could really do something!

But, the moment that the door closed, she forgot her feeling of victory, for, of a sudden, she saw Dr. Blanchard in a new light. She saw him lay the little figure upon the bed - she saw him pull off his coat. And then, while she held the basin of water, she saw him get to work. And as she watched him her last feeling of doubt was swept away.

"He may say that he's not interested in people," she told herself joyously, "but he is. He may think that he doesn't care for religion - but he does. There's love of people in every move of his hands! There's something religious in the very way his fingers touch Lily!"

Yes, she was seeing the Young Doctor in a new light. As she watched him she knew that he had quite forgotten her presence - had quite forgotten the little quarrels that had all but ruined their chance at friendship. She knew that his mind was only on the child who lay so still under his hands - she knew that all the intensity of his nature was concentrated upon Lily. As she watched him, deftly obeying His simple directions, she gloried in his skill - in his surety.

And then, at last, Lily opened her eyes. She might have

been waking from a deep slumber as she opened them - she might have been dreaming a pleasant dream as she smiled faintly. Rose-Marie had a sudden feeling - a feeling that she had experienced before - that the child was seeing visions, with her great sightless eyes, that other, normal folk could not see. All at once a great dread clutched at her soul.

"She's not dying -?" she whispered, gaspingly. "Her smile is so very - wonderful. She's not dying?"

The Young Doctor turned swiftly from the bed. All at once he looked like a knight to Rose-Marie - an armourless, modern knight who fought an endless fight against the dragons of disease and pain.

"Bless your heart, no!" he answered. "She isn't dying! We'll bring her around in a few minutes. And now" - a great tenderness shone out of his eyes, "tell me all about it. You were very sketchy," his gesture indicated the other room, "out there! How did the child really get hurt - and how did you come to be here? How - Why, Rose-Marie.... *Sweetheart*!"

For Rose-Marie had fainted very quietly - and for the first time in all of her strong young life.

XIX

AND THE HAPPY ENDING

They were sitting together at the luncheon table - the Superintendent, Rose-Marie, and the Young Doctor. The noontime sunshine slanted across the table - dancing on the silver, touching softly Rose-Marie's curls, finding an answering sparkle in the Young Doctor's smile. And silence - the warm silence of happiness - lay over them all.

It was the Young Doctor who spoke first.

"Just about a month ago, it was," he said reflectively, "that I saw Lily for the first time. And now" - he paused teasingly - "and now -"

Rose-Marie laid down the bit of roll that she was buttering. Her face was glowing with eagerness.

"They've come to some decision," she whispered, in a question that was little more than a breath of sound, "the doctors at the hospital have come to some decision?"

The Superintendent was leaning forward and her kind soul shone out of her tired eyes. "Tell us at once, Billy Blanchard!" she ordered, "*At once!*"

Quite after the maddening fashion of men the Young Doctor did not answer - not until he had consumed, and appreciatively, the bit of roll that he had been buttering. And then - "The other doctors agree with my diagnosis," he told them simply. "It's an extraordinary case, they say; but a not incurable one. The shock - when Jim kicked her - was a blessing in disguise. Not, of course, that I'd prescribe kicks for crippled children! But" - the term that he used was long and technical - "but such things have happened. Not often, of course. The doctors agree with me that, if her voice comes back - as I believe it will - there may be a very real hope for her hearing. And her eyes " - his voice was suddenly tender - "well - thousands of slum kiddies are blind - and thousands of them have been cured. If Lily is, some day, a normal child - if she can some day speak and see, and hear, it will be -"

The Superintendent's voice was soft -

"It is already a miracle!" she said simply. "It is already a miracle. Look at Jim - working for a small salary, *and liking it*! Look at Bennie - he was the head of his class in school, this month, he told me. And Ella -"

The Young Doctor interrupted.

"Ella and her mother went to church with us last Sunday," he said. "Rose-Marie and I were starting out, together, and they asked if they might go along. I tell you" - his eyes were looking deep, *deep*, into the eyes of Rose-Marie and he spoke directly to her, "I tell you, dear - I've learned a great many lessons in the last few weeks. Jim isn't the only one - or Bennie. Lily isn't the only nearly incurable case that has found new strength...."

Rose-Marie was blushing. The Superintendent, watching the waves of colour sweep over her face, spoke suddenly - reminiscently.

"Child," she said - and laughter, tremulous laughter, was in her voice, "your face is ever so *pink*! I believe," she was quoting, "'that you have a best beau'!'"

The Young Doctor was laughing, too. Strangely enough his laughter had just the suggestion of a tremor in it.

"I'll say that she has!" he replied, and his words, though slangy, were very tender. "I'll say that she has!" And then - "Are *we* going back to the little town, Rose-Marie," he questioned. "Are *we* going back to the little town to be married?"

The blush had died from Rose-Marie's face, leaving it just faintly flushed. The eyes that she raised to the Young Doctor's eyes were like warm stars.

"No," she told him, "we're not! I've thought it all out. We're going to be married here - here in the Settlement House. I'll write for my aunts to come on - and for my old pastor! I couldn't be married without my aunts.... And my pastor; he christened me, and he welcomed me into the church, and" - all at once she started up from the table, "I'm going up-stairs to write, now," she managed. "I want to tell them that we're going to start our home here" - her voice broke, "here, on our own Island...." Like a flash she was out of the door.

The Young Doctor was on his feet. Luncheon was quite forgotten.

Margaret E. Sangster

"I think," he said softly, and his face was like a light, "I think that I'll go with her - and help her with the letter!" The door closed, sharply, upon his hurrying back.

*　　*　　*　　*　　*

The Superintendent, left alone at the table, rang for the maid. Her voice was carefully calm as she ordered the evening meal. But her eyes were just a bit misty as she looked into the maid's dull face.

"Mrs. Volsky," she said suddenly, "love must have its way! And love is -"

The maid looked at her blankly. Obviously she did not understand. But, seeing her neat apron, her clean hands, her carefully combed hair, one could forgive her vague expression.

"What say?" she questioned.

The Superintendent laughed wearily, "Anyway," she remarked, "Ella likes her work, doesn't she? And Jim? And Bennie is going to be a great man, some day - isn't he? And Lily may be made well - quite well! You should be a glad woman, Mrs. Volsky!"

Pride flamed up, suddenly, in the maid's face – blotting out the dullness.

"God," she said simply and - marvel of marvels - her usually toneless voice was athrob with love - "God is good!" She went out, with a tray full of dishes.

Her chin in the palm of her hand, the Superintendent

stared off into space. If she was thinking of a little blond child - lying in a hospital bed - if she was thinking of a man with sleek hair, trying to make a new start - if she was thinking of a girl with dark, flashing eyes, and a small, grubby-fingered boy, her expression did not mirror her thought. Only once she spoke, as she was folding her napkin. And then -

"They're both very young," she murmured, a shade wistfully. Perhaps she was remembering the springtime of her own youth.

Choose from Thousands of 1stWorldLibrary Classics By

Adolphus WilliamWard
Aesop
Agatha Christie
Alexander Aaronsohn
Alexander Kielland
Alexandre Dumas
Alfred Gatty
Alfred Ollivant
Alice Duer Miller
Alice Turner Curtis
Alice Dunbar
Ambrose Bierce
Amelia E. Barr
Andrew Lang
Andrew McFarland Davis
Anna Sewell
Annie Besant
Annie Hamilton Donnell
Annie Payson Call
Anton Chekhov
Arnold Bennett
Arthur Conan Doyle
Arthur Ransome
Atticus
B. M. Bower
Basil King
Bayard Taylor
Ben Macomber
Booth Tarkington
Bram Stoker
C. Collodi
C. E. Orr
C. M. Ingleby
Carolyn Wells
Catherine Parr Traill
Charles A. Eastman
Charles Dickens
Charles Dudley Warner
Charles Farrar Browne
Charles Ives
Charles Kingsley
Charles Lathrop Pack
Charles Whibley
Charles Willing Beale
Charlotte M. Braeme
Charlotte M.Yonge
Clair W. Hayes
Clarence Day Jr.
Clarence E. Mulford

Clemence Housman
Confucius
Cornelis DeWitt Wilcox
Cyril Burleigh
D. H. Lawrence
Daniel Defoe
David Garnett
Don Carlos Janes
Donald Keyhole
Dorothy Kilner
Dougan Clark
E. Nesbit
E.P.Roe
E. Phillips Oppenheim
Edgar Allan Poe
Edgar Rice Burroughs
Edith Wharton
Edward J. O'Biren
John Cournos
Edwin L. Arnold
Eleanor Atkins
Elizabeth Cleghorn
Gaskell
Elizabeth Von Arnim
Ellem Key
Emily Dickinson
Erasmus W. Jones
Ernie Howard Pie
Ethel Turner
Ethel Watts Mumford
Eugenie Foa
Eugene Wood
Evelyn Everett-Green
Everard Cotes
F. J. Cross
Federick Austin Ogg
Ferdinand Ossendowski
Francis Bacon
Francis Darwin
Frances Hodgson Burnett
Frank Gee Patchin
Frank Harris
Frank Jewett Mather
Frank L. Packard
Frederick Trevor Hill
Frederick Winslow Taylor
Friedrich Kerst
Friedrich Nietzsche
Fyodor Dostoyevsky

Gabrielle E. Jackson
Garrett P. Serviss
Gaston Leroux
George Ade
Geroge Bernard Shaw
George Ebers
George Eliot
George MacDonald
George Orwell
George Tucker
George W. Cable
George Wharton James
Gertrude Atherton
Grace E. King
Grant Allen
Guillermo A. Sherwell
Gulielma Zollinger
Gustav Flaubert
H. A. Cody
H. B. Irving
H. G. Wells
H. H. Munro
H. Irving Hancock
H. Rider Haggard
H. W. C. Davis
Hamilton Wright Mabie
Hans Christian Andersen
Harold Avery
Harold McGrath
Harriet Beecher Stowe
Harry Houidini
Helent Hunt Jackson
Helen Nicolay
Hendy David Thoreau
Henrik Ibsen
Henry Adams
Henry Ford
Henry Frost
Henry James
Henry Jones Ford
Henry Seton Merriman
Henry Wadsworth
Longfellow
Henry W Longfellow
Herbert A. Giles
Herbert N. Casson
Herman Hesse
Homer
Honore De Balzac

Horace Walpole
Horatio Alger, Jr.
Howard Pyle
Howard R. Garis
Hugh Lofting
Hugh Walpole
Humphry Ward
Ian Maclaren
Israel Abrahams
J.G.Austin
J. Henri Fabre
J. M. Barrie
J. Macdonald Oxley
J. S. Knowles
J. Storer Clouston
Jack London
Jacob Abbott
James Allen
James Lane Allen
James Andrews
James Baldwin
James DeMille
James Joyce
James Oliver Curwood
James Oppenheim
James Otis
Jane Austen
Jens Peter Jacobsen
Jerome K. Jerome
John Burroughs
John F. Kennedy
John Gay
John Glasworthy
John Habberton
John Joy Bell
John Milton
John Philip Sousa
Jonathan Swift
Joseph Carey
Joseph Conrad
Joseph Jacobs
Julian Hawthrone
Julies Vernes
Justin Huntly McCarthy
Kakuzo Okakura
Kenneth Grahame
Kate Langley Bosher
L. A. Abbot
L. T. Meade
L. Frank Baum
Laura Lee Hope

Laurence Housman
Leo Tolstoy
Leonid Andreyev
Lewis Carroll
Lilian Bell
Lloyd Osbourne
Louis Tracy
Louisa May Alcott
Lucy Fitch Perkins
Lucy Maud Montgomery
Lydia Miller Middleton
Lyndon Orr
M. H. Adams
Margaret E. Sangster
Margaret Vandercook
Maria Edgeworth
Maria Thompson Daviess
Mariano Azuela
Marion Polk Angellotti
Mark Overton
Mark Twain
Mary Austin
Mary Cole
Mary Rowlandson
Mary Wollstonecraft
Shelley
Max Beerbohm
Myra Kelly
Nathaniel Hawthrone
O. F. Walton
Oscar Wilde
Owen Johnson
P.G.Wodehouse
Paul and Mable Thorn
Paul G. Tomlinson
Paul Severing
Peter B. Kyne
Plato
R. Derby Holmes
R. L. Stevenson
Rabindranath Tagore
Rahul Alvares
Ralph Waldo Emmerson
Rene Descartes
Rex E. Beach
Richard Harding Davis
Richard Jefferies
Robert Barr
Robert Frost
Robert Gordon Anderson
Robert L. Drake

Robert Lansing
Robert Michael Ballantyne
Robert W. Chambers
Rosa Nouchette Carey
Ross Kay
Rudyard Kipling
Samuel B. Allison
Samuel Hopkins Adams
Sarah Bernhardt
Selma Lagerlof
Sherwood Anderson
Sigmund Freud
Standish O'Grady
Stanley Weyman
Stella Benson
Stephen Crane
Stewart Edward White
Stijn Streuvels
Swami Abhedananda
Swami Parmananda
T. S. Ackland
The Princess Der Ling
Thomas A. Janvier
Thomas A Kempis
Thomas Anderton
Thomas Bailey Aldrich
Thomas Bulfinch
Thomas De Quincey
Thomas H. Huxley
Thomas Hardy
Thomas More
Thornton W. Burgess
U. S. Grant
Valentine Williams
Victor Appleton
Virginia Woolf
Walter Scott
Washington Irving
Wilbur Lawton
Wilkie Collins
Willa Cather
Willard F. Baker
William Makepeace
Thackeray
William W. Walter
Winston Churchill
Yei Theodora Ozaki
Young E. Allison
Zane Grey